St Elizabeth's Children's Hospital London

Dealing with sick kids can be heartbreaking,
funny, and uplifting, often all at once!

This series takes a look at a hospital set up
especially to deal with such children,
peeping behind the scenes into almost all the
departments and clinics, exploring the
problems and solutions of various diseases,
while watching the staff fall helplessly
in love—with the kids and with each other.

Enjoy!

D1634383

Jennifer Taylor has been writing Mills & Boon®
romances for some time, but only recently 'discovered'
Medical Romances™. She was so captivated by these
heart-warming stories that she immediately set out to
write them herself! As a former librarian who worked
in scientific and industrial research, Jennifer enjoys the
research involved with the writing of each book, as
well as the chance it gives her to create a cast of
wonderful new characters. When not writing or doing
research for her latest book, Jennifer's hobbies include
reading, travel, and walking her dog. She lives in the
north-west of England with her husband and children.

SMALL MIRACLES

JENNIFER TAYLOR

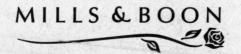

MILLS & BOON

First published in Great Britain 2000
Harlequin Mills & Boon Limited,
Eton House, 18-24 Paradise Road, Richmond, Surrey TW9 1SR

© Jennifer Taylor 2000

ISBN 0 263 82429 2

Set in Times Roman 10½ on 11 pt.
112-0006-61903

Printed and bound in Spain
by Litografía Rosés S.A., Barcelona

CHAPTER ONE

THE little boy had been standing with his nose pressed against the window for well over five minutes now.

Staff Nurse Lucy Benson finished cleaning the nasogastric feeding tube attached to two-week-old Jade Jackson and closed the portholes in the side of the incubator as she cast him another glance. So far she hadn't seen anyone with him and she couldn't help wondering who he was. There had been two new admissions during the night to the neonatal intensive care unit of St Elizabeth's Children's Hospital, where she worked, so maybe he was the brother of one of her new charges.

'He's here!'

Megan Whittaker, who worked part-time on the unit, had come up behind her and Lucy jumped.

'What do you mean? Who's here?' she demanded, turning to look at the other woman with puzzled brown eyes.

Megan rolled her eyes. 'Who do you think? The new man, of course! Rumour had it that he was coming to look round today and I just saw Martyn Lennard ushering someone into the office when I went for my break. It has to be him! Have you found out his name yet, Lucy?'

Lucy shook her head so that her bob of pale blonde hair bounced around her pretty, heart-shaped face. 'Nope. I'm as much in the dark as everyone else, I'm afraid.'

She sighed as she went to wash her hands. 'It's been a real mess, hasn't it? I mean, they'd no sooner appointed someone to the consultant paediatrician's post than the next we heard was that he'd had a heart attack and wouldn't be able to take it up.'

'I know. And he's only forty, too. Same age as my Jim.'

Megan shuddered expressively. 'You just never know what's going to happen, do you? Still, at least they found someone to replace him straight away. We'd have been really stuck if they'd had to go through all the interviews and short-listing again, especially as it happened right in the middle of Christmas and the New Year.'

'We would indeed. And, from what I can gather, it was a toss-up who got the job in the first place, so there's no question of him being second best,' Lucy agreed.

She dried her hands then glanced towards the window again and frowned as she saw that the little boy was still there. 'Who is that child, Megan? Do you know?'

Megan shrugged. 'No idea. Probably the brother of one of the two new babies who came in last night, I expect.'

'That's what I thought.' Lucy smiled as she watched the little boy move closer to the glass, obviously fascinated by what was going on inside the unit. 'He's a real little poppet, isn't he? Just look at that gorgeous curly black hair and those big grey eyes.'

'Mmm, I wonder if he takes after his daddy,' Megan suggested with a meaningful grin.

Lucy laughed. 'You are incorrigible! I thought you were a happily married woman?'

'I am! I wouldn't swap my Jim for the world. But even if you're on a diet it doesn't mean that you can't enjoy looking at the menu, does it? Anyway, that's rich coming from ''Love 'em and leave 'em'' Lucy!'

Lucy chuckled as Megan hurried away to check on baby Jack Williams as the alarm on his incubator sounded a warning. It was impossible to take offence at her friend's teasing when it had been meant purely in fun.

Megan had coined the nickname more out of despair than anything else, unable to understand why Lucy never went out with anyone for more than a few weeks, and it had stuck. It was never used nastily, mainly because she took care that nobody got hurt.

If she went out with a man then she made sure that he

knew the rules. At the first hint that he might be getting too serious then she tactfully broke things off. The last thing she wanted was to hurt anyone by her decision to avoid any kind of permanent commitment.

Now she pushed the remark to the back of her mind as she did a quick visual check on the babies, starting with Jack Williams. He had been born three weeks prematurely and was being monitored for sleep apnoea, a worrying condition whereby he stopped breathing during his sleep. However, she could see that he had started breathing again spontaneously so there was no need to panic.

Sister Thomas was on holiday and wouldn't be back until the end of the month so it was Lucy's responsibility to keep a check on things in her absence, although all the staff were so highly trained that they needed little supervision.

There were ten babies in the unit at present, which was almost their limit. Babies were admitted to the neo-natal intensive care unit if they were suffering from a medical condition which made it imperative that they received skilled round-the-clock care.

Some were very sick, like tiny Abigail Foster, born two days earlier with spina bifida. She was barely holding her own and Lucy knew that the next day or so would be critical for her.

There was a lot of stress involved with the job, and sometimes heartache, yet she knew that she wouldn't trade places with anyone. The joy of finally handing over a healthy baby to its parents and knowing that she had played a vital role in its recovery was the best feeling in the world. It helped make up in some little way for the fact that she would never experience the joy of holding her own child in her arms.

She sighed as she wondered where that thought had sprung from. She glanced towards the window again, wondering if it had been seeing the little boy which had prompted it. However, there was no sign of him now so she determinedly shook off the feeling of melancholy

which had beset her. She had a lot in her life to be grateful
for so she would think about that!

'I'll go for my break now, Megan, seeing as everything
is quiet,' she informed the older woman as she went to join
her by baby Williams' incubator. 'Lauren and Sandra are
back so there's plenty of cover,' she continued, referring to
the two other nurses on duty that day. With a staff of five
on the day shift, including Sister Thomas, they were pretty
well staffed although there was always plenty to keep them
busy.

'Fine. Oh, and try to find out something about the new
bloke, will you? His name and where he worked before
would be a start,' Megan declared plaintively. 'I can't believe the grapevine has let us down so badly that we don't
have a clue who he is!'

'I'll try, but bear in mind that I happen to be a staff nurse
not an MI5 agent,' Lucy retorted dryly. 'I never thought to
bring my dark glasses and funny hat with me this morning,
so don't hold out too many hopes!'

She hurried away as Megan laughed, pausing only to
shed her apron before leaving the unit. Their uniform con-
sisted of comfortable white cotton tops and black trousers,
over which they wore brightly coloured aprons printed with
nursery characters when they were doing any messy jobs.

It was always so warm in the intensive care unit that
thicker clothing would have been unbearable to work in.
With her well-rounded figure and not overly generous five
feet three inches of height, Lucy was aware that the outfit
wasn't perhaps the most flattering, but she found it both
comfortable and practical. She also knew that it helped put
the parents at ease dealing with someone who didn't appear
too starchy. Those advantages far outweighed anything
else, to her mind.

Now as she hurried to the lift she felt in the pocket of
her trousers for some change, groaning as she realised that
she had forgotten to bring any with her. She was just turning back to get some money out of her purse when the

office door opened and Martyn Lennard, the hospital manager, appeared.

'Ah, Lucy, I was just coming to find you. I wanted to introduce you to our new paediatric consultant.' He smiled as a second man came out of the room. 'This is Tom Farrell who will be joining us officially as from tomorrow. And very pleased to have him we are, too!'

Lucy had no time to gather her scattered wits, although how she would have done that given even a month's notice she had no idea! She could feel the shock running from the top of her head right down to the tips of her toes as she stared at the dark-haired man in front of her.

'Hello, Lucy. This is a surprise. How are you?'

His voice was very deep and there was no way that she could miss the undercurrent it held. Obviously Tom wasn't lying when he said it was a surprise to see her and just as obviously it wasn't a pleasant one either!

She took a quick breath to steady her racing heartbeat but it was impossible to keep the quaver out of her voice. 'F...f...fine, thank you. H...how are you, Tom?'

'Very well.' He had himself under control once again as he turned to Martyn Lennard, who was listening curiously to the exchange. 'Lucy and I know one another from way back,' he informed the other man calmly. 'We worked together in Derbyshire...oh, about five years ago now, wasn't it, Lucy?'

'Er...yes, about that,' she agreed quickly, trying to ignore the pang she felt. Tom had made it sound as though they had been nothing more than colleagues in those days, but they had been a lot more than that!

She hastily averted her eyes as he turned to her once more, determined not to let him see how it had stung to hear him refer to the past so dismissively. It shouldn't have done, of course. Five years and no contact between them since should have destroyed any feelings she'd had. It was the fact that she felt something even now which worried her most of all.

'Martyn has been giving me the grand tour. I must say that I'm impressed with the set-up here.' He gave her a cool smile, his grey eyes betraying nothing more than polite interest when she looked at him.

'Have you worked here ever since you left Derbyshire? I can't recall you mentioning exactly where you were moving to, now that I think about it. All you said was something about going down south, if I'm not mistaken.'

He wasn't mistaken. And the fact that he recalled what she'd said was a small sop to her bruised feelings, although she carefully kept all trace of emotion from her voice as she replied to the question.

'I started working here about six months after I left Derbyshire. It was what I always wanted to do, to work with babies.'

'So I recall.' There was a huskiness to his deep voice which sent a shiver racing through her body. Lucy didn't hear what Martyn Lennard said then as she struggled to control it, but it wasn't easy.

She let her gaze linger on Tom as he turned to the other man, drinking in the changes five years had wrought with an urgency she couldn't understand. It shouldn't have mattered whether or not he had changed in that time but she felt a sudden need to fill in all the blank spaces.

At first sight he appeared much the same as he had always done, she decided. His thick, dark hair was untouched by any sign of grey and his rangy six-foot frame looked as lean as ever—or maybe even a little leaner, if her memory wasn't playing tricks?

She frowned as she suddenly noticed how his suit jacket seemed to hang rather loosely on him, as though he might have lost weight in recent months. Her frown grew deeper as her gaze moved to the newly angular contours of his face. There were lines on it which certainly hadn't been there five years before, a new solemnity about his expression which seemed at odds with the man she recalled. Tom had always possessed an overwhelming zest for life and one of the things she remembered best about him was his humour. Yet there seemed little sign of it in the grave-faced man before her now. It made her wonder what had happened to him in the intervening years…

'Daddy, me thirsty. Me have a drink, please?'

Lucy started as a child suddenly appeared from the office. It was the little boy who had been looking through the window earlier and she felt a band of pain grip her heart as she realised that he must be Tom's son. He could be no more than three years old but, now that she knew who he was, she immediately saw the resemblance. The child had the same deep grey eyes as his father had, the same springy hair with a tendency to curl, although his was a shade darker than Tom's mahogany brown colour. When he gave her a shy smile she had to bite her lip as she saw the dimple which appeared in his left cheek.

How many times had she teased Tom about *his* dimple, playing shamelessly on the fact that he had hated it?

'Lucy?'

She jumped as she realised that Martyn Lennard was speaking to her. A wash of colour ran up her face as she saw Tom look at her. She steadfastly avoided his eyes as she turned to the older man. The last thing she wanted was for Tom to guess where her thoughts had been wandering just now!

'I'm sorry, what was that?'

Martyn smiled understandingly. He was a pleasant-faced man in his late forties with neatly cut salt-and-pepper hair and a brisk manner which didn't disguise his genuine commitment to the hospital and its staff. 'I expect it's been a bit of a surprise meeting up with Tom like this, hasn't it?'

He didn't seem to expect her to say anything, thankfully enough, and carried on. 'I take it that you were on your way to the canteen when I stopped you, so why don't you show Tom the way so that he can grab a cup of coffee and get Adam here a drink? There are a few phone calls I need to make so it will give us both time to get sorted out.'

He checked his watch then turned to Tom. 'See you back here in about twenty minutes, if that's OK? Then we can continue our tour.'

He hurried off, leaving behind a small silence broken when little Adam said hopefully, 'Drink of juice, Daddy…please.'

'OK, tiger.' Tom ruffled the child's hair, then looked at Lucy with a faint lift of his brows. 'Do you mind showing us how to get to the canteen? I haven't had chance to get fully acquainted with the layout as yet.'

'Of…of course.' Lucy hurriedly led the way to the lifts, pressing the button to summon one as Tom and Adam came to join her. She gave the little boy a quick smile as he looked up at her with solemn grey eyes, feeling the pain pinching her heart again.

Why did it hurt so much to know that what she had always expected had happened? Tom had never made any secret of the fact that he'd wanted children so she shouldn't be surprised. Yet it hurt in a way she wouldn't have be-lieved possible to know that he had found what he'd wanted with another woman.

She quickly curtailed that thought. She had done her share of heart-searching over the years and it was pointless letting herself dwell on something which couldn't be changed.

'So, Adam, what's your favourite juice?' she asked brightly instead. 'Orange or blackcurrant?'

'Apple,' Adam declared firmly. 'Adam likes apple juice.'

'I like apple juice, too,' she told him, smiling as he grinned happily at her although her heart seemed to ache even harder. With his tousled black curls and huge grey eyes, he was utterly adorable and she felt a swift pang of envy for his mother. How she would have loved to have had a child like this, to have had Tom's son, if only it had been possible.

She turned away as the lift arrived, blinking back the tears which had misted her eyes at that thought. She had made her decision five years ago and obviously it had been the right one. She should be glad, not sad, that Tom had got what he'd always wanted.

'Which floor?'

She looked round as Tom reminded her that he had no idea where they were going, the colour running up her cheeks as she saw the questioning look he gave her. Would he guess what was wrong with her? she wondered shakily, then inwardly sighed. Of course not! The days when they were so attuned that they could communicate without words were long gone. Now he had someone else to share his thoughts—and everything else!—with.

'Sixth. The staff canteen and rest rooms are up there along with most of the offices,' she explained flatly, less comforted by that thought than she should have been.

'I suppose I'll get used to all these floors in time, but it's a big change after the last place I worked.' Tom pressed the button and the lift doors glided shut as he turned to her.

Lucy smoothed her features into a suitably bland expression. 'Oh, and where was that?' She gave a short laugh, hating to hear the note of strain it held even now. 'I'm afraid the hospital grapevine let us down this time because we had no idea who'd been appointed to the post, let alone where you'd been working before, you see.'

'So I gathered,' he replied dryly. 'I realised how shocked you were to see me just now, Lucy.' He shrugged, his wide shoulders rising and falling beneath the too-loose jacket. 'I expect I was the last person you ever hoped to bump into again?'

She had no time to think up a reply as they reached their floor just then and the lift came to a stop. Tom took hold of Adam's hand and drew him to one side so that she could lead the way. She walked swiftly along the corridor to the brightly lit canteen, conscious of two sets of grey eyes focused on her back. It made her very self-conscious as she wondered what Tom was thinking—if he was noticing the changes the years had surely brought about in her.

Did she look older, fatter, maybe more lined? she wondered before she could stop herself. Crazy and pointless though it was, she couldn't help wondering what he thought of her now and if...if he still found her attractive!

She took a quick breath before she turned, struggling to rid her mind of such nonsense. 'The canteen is self-service but the food is very good. You'll find that most of the staff eat here. Martyn Lennard managed to persuade one of the top chefs to work out the menus, so standards are high,' she explained carefully.

'Bit of a change from the usual canteen fare, then, I imagine.' Tom suddenly grinned so that his whole face lit up, the dimple she recalled flashing in and out of his lean cheek. 'I take it that cheese pie isn't on the menu?'

Lucy couldn't help laughing at that. 'Do you remember how awful it was? I don't know what the cooks did to it but I've never seen anything like it since—'

'Stringy cheese in soggy pastry with a puddle of oil floating on top,' Tom put in, chuckling deeply. 'Then there was the lumpy mashed potato to go with it. Yum!'

Lucy groaned. 'Don't! I used to dread Fridays when it was the dish of the day. I have nightmares even now thinking about it. Obviously, it's stuck in your mind, too!'

'There is a lot I remember about those days, Lucy,' he said softly with an inflection in his voice which brought her eyes winging to his face.

She took a quick breath but it did nothing to still the sudden pounding of her heart as she looked into his eyes and saw there the evidence that he was telling the truth. Tom *did* remember what had gone on between them even though he might have chosen to gloss over it for Martyn Lennard's benefit. It was a relief when a small voice suddenly piped up and broke the increasingly uncomfortable silence.

'Juice, Daddy. Please!'

'Sorry, Adam. I'll go and get you some straight away.' Tom's voice was level once more, making Lucy wonder if she'd imagined what had happened. However, when he turned to her there was something in the depths of his eyes still which told her that it hadn't been imagination at all.

Tom was as disturbed as she was by this unexpected encounter. It was both a relief and yet deeply unsettling to realise it. Would they be able to work together without the spectre of the past intruding all the time? she wondered. Only time would tell.

'So what would you like, Lucy? Coffee?' he asked politely.

'Yes, thank you. But you don't need to get it. I'll get my own,' she began before suddenly remembering that she didn't have any money with her. She flushed uncomfortably, wondering how best to explain her predicament without making an issue out of it. However, Tom merely shrugged.

'I think I can run to an extra cup of coffee, so don't worry about it.' He glanced round the room and nodded to an empty table near the window. 'How about taking Adam over there while I fetch the drinks?'

He headed for the counter, leaving her little option but to do as he'd said. Lucy bit back a sigh as she turned to Adam with a rather forced smile. 'Shall we go and sit down while Daddy gets our drinks?'

The little boy looked uncertainly at her for a second then nodded gravely. However, Lucy noticed how his head kept swivelling round while he checked that Tom was still in sight as they crossed the room. There were staff there from several different departments, having their breaks. Lucy nodded to those she knew as she guided Adam between the tables. St Elizabeth's was a big place and it was impossible to keep completely up to date with everyone who worked there, although, for a hospital set right in the heart of London, the turnover of staff was surprisingly low.

Lucy knew that most people stayed because they felt the same way about the job as she did. Helping sick children was possibly the most demanding and yet the most rewarding work any of them could do, and at Lizzie's, as the hospital was affectionately called by those who worked there, the level of care and commitment to the welfare of each child was high. Everyone who worked there prided him or herself on giving one hundred per cent.

'And who's this you've got with you?' Dave Lennox, a charge nurse on Orthopaedics, asked as they passed his table. Lucy paused, laying a restraining hand on Adam's shoulder so that he wouldn't wander off.

'This is Adam. He's come up here to have a drink of juice, haven't you, love?'

'Apple juice,' Adam agreed solemnly. 'Adam likes apple juice.'

'Good for you. It will make you grow into a big strong boy, won't it?' Dave winked at the little boy then turned to Lucy with a frown. 'I didn't know that you had kids, Lucy?'

'I...I don't.' She took a quick breath, trying to control the pain which seemed to lance straight through her heart. 'Adam isn't my little boy. He's the son of the new paediatric consultant, Tom Farrell.'

'Oh, I see. I *thought* you'd been keeping it very quiet.' Dave laughed off his mistake and she summoned a smile before she carried on towards the empty table, although her heart was aching. Nobody knew that she couldn't have children because she'd never spoken about it, so Dave couldn't have guessed how his remark had hurt. Maybe it shouldn't have done because she'd long since come to terms with the situation.

She had been fifteen when the doctors had told her there was little chance that she would have children of her own. At the time she had barely taken in what they'd been saying. It had been much later that it had hit her, when she had met Tom and discovered how much he had wanted a family, that she had understood fully what it meant. Now as she helped Adam climb onto a chair she felt angry at having been dealt such a bitter blow by fate. Her life could have been so different but for that!

'Right, here we go—apple juice for Adam, coffee for Lucy and tea for me.'

Tom set the tray on the table then doled out their drinks. He leant over to help Adam slot the tiny plastic straw into the hole in the container of apple juice, sighing as the little boy promptly moved it out of reach.

'Me do,' Adam declared, his tongue peeping between his lips as he struggled to pierce the seal on the carton.

'He's so independent,' Tom said ruefully. 'He's only three but to hear him sometimes you'd think he was ninety-three!'

Lucy laughed as she looked at the little boy. 'He's doing very well, aren't you, Adam?' She placed a guiding finger against the end of the straw to help it slot into place. 'There. Well done!'

She turned to Tom again as the child took a thirsty swallow of his juice, and felt her smile fade as she saw the expression on his face, a mixture of regret and such longing that her heart seemed to turn inside out.

She looked away, deliberately closing her mind to the reason why he had looked at her like that. It was none of her business. She had given up any right to wonder about things like that five years ago!

'So what made you apply for this job, Tom?' she asked instead. 'Didn't it come as a bit of a wrench leaving Derbyshire after all this time?'

'I left there some years ago,' he replied flatly. 'A couple of months after you did, in fact.'

'Really?' She couldn't hide her surprise. 'But you were so happy there…' She tailed off, wishing she hadn't said that, but it was impossible to take it back.

'I was—very happy.' His face was devoid of expression as he picked up his cup. 'However, situations change, don't they?'

Was he saying that he hadn't been happy once she had

left? No matter how foolish it was, Lucy felt her heart lift at the thought.

'...a real dream of a job, of course. Florida is such a wonderful place both to live and work.'

She suddenly realised what he had said and raised startled brown eyes to his face. 'Florida? That's where you went to work after Derbyshire?'

'Uh-huh. It was the offer of a lifetime and I'd have been a fool to turn it down. Fiona and I brought our wedding forward and we went over there straight after we got married.'

'I see. It must have been marvellous, a...a wonderful opportunity, as you say,' Lucy said woodenly, struggling to hide her dismay. It seemed incredible that she could have forgotten about his wife with Adam sitting beside her, but she had!

She looked down at the table, afraid of what he might see on her face at that moment. She didn't need to be a mathematician to work out the logistics because he'd already explained that he had left Derbyshire only months after she had. Obviously, it hadn't taken him long to meet someone else and decide to marry her, had it?

'It was. However, Fiona found it very hard to settle over there. She became increasingly homesick, especially after we had Adam and she found it difficult to get out and about as much.'

She took a quick breath, determined that he would never know how hurt she felt that he had fallen in love with another woman so quickly. It was what she had hoped would happen, in all honesty. She had wanted Tom to be happy but, perversely, it still hurt. 'I expect it was hard for her, having a new baby to look after and being so far away from her friends and family?'

'I imagine so.' Tom shrugged as he took a sip of his tea. 'Anyway, we decided to come back to England in the end and moved to Cornwall. I got a job in a hospital just outside Truro, and probably would have stayed there if it hadn't been for Adam and all the problems I've had trying to find someone to look after him this past year.'

Lucy felt as though she were wading through quicksand all of a sudden. What did Tom mean about finding someone to look after Adam? Where was his mother? She was dying to ask and yet at the same time she was afraid that he might read too much into it. She was still trying to decide what to do when he carried on and she had the funniest feeling that he wanted her to hear the full story for some reason.

'It wasn't so bad in the summer, of course. Cornwall is such a beautiful part of the world that I was able to take my pick of any number of suitable applicants for the job of Adam's nanny.' He sighed heavily. 'However, it's less appealing living there in the middle of winter. Most young girls want a bit of excitement in their lives and we lived rather too far outside the town to make nights out there a viable proposition.

'The last nanny Adam had stayed only three days then handed in her notice because she said it was too quiet and she couldn't stand it. I realised then that if I wanted any kind of continuity of care for him I would have to move to the city. When this post came up it seemed like the ideal solution, even though I didn't think I'd got it at first.'

Lucy couldn't contain herself any longer. Not that there seemed any reason to, because he appeared quite willing to tell her everything she wanted to know. 'But why do you need a nanny? I don't understand.' She glanced at the little boy and automatically lowered her voice. 'Where is Adam's mother, Tom? Why isn't she looking after him herself?'

Tom looked down at the table so that it was impossible to see his expression clearly. 'Fiona died just over a year ago in a car crash. I've been bringing Adam up by myself since then. Apart from the nannies, it's been just the two of us.'

He suddenly looked up and there was such finality in his voice when he continued that it made her go cold. 'And that's the way I intend it to remain. Adam and I don't need anyone else in our lives.'

CHAPTER TWO

'HE'S a widower, evidently. His wife died in a car crash about a year ago. He has a little boy, too. Dave Lennox was just telling me on the way up in the lift. Such a shame, isn't it?' Lauren Jacobs finished changing into her uniform and closed her locker door. She turned to Lucy, her pretty face alight with curiosity.

'Is it right what Dave said, that you and Tom Farrell knew one another when you both worked in Derbyshire? Martyn Lennard mentioned it when he was showing Dr Farrell round Orthopaedics yesterday.'

'That's right. Small world, isn't it?' Lucy fixed a smile to her lips, praying that the younger girl wouldn't guess how she was feeling, yet how *did* she feel? Surely the shock of discovering that Tom was the new paediatric consultant should have worn off by now? After all she'd had twenty-four hours to absorb the impact it had made on her yet she knew in her heart that she still hadn't come to terms with what had happened, or with what Tom had said in the canteen the previous day.

Was that why she felt so on edge at the thought of seeing him today—the way he had stated so categorically that he didn't need anyone in his life apart from his son? Surely Tom hadn't felt it necessary to impress on her that he wasn't interested in taking up where they had left off five years before?

'You kept that very quiet, Lucy. You never mentioned that you knew this Tom Farrell when I asked you about him yesterday.' Megan gave her a considering look as Lauren left the room. 'How come?'

Lucy shrugged as she picked up a clean apron and

21

slipped it over her head. 'It didn't seem that important. It was a long time ago, after all.'

She checked her watch then walked swiftly to the door to put a stop to any more questions. 'Sister Carmichael will be waiting to give me her report. I'd better not keep her.'

The staff room door slammed shut and she breathed a sigh of relief at being let off so lightly as she hurried along the corridor. She was fond of Megan but the other woman was a dreadful gossip and she didn't want any rumours flying around about her and Tom...

She grimaced as she realised how unlikely that was. Nobody but them knew what had happened five years ago and it was highly unlikely that Tom was going to mention it! There would be no gossip for the simple reason that there wasn't anything to gossip about.

Ten minutes later, having heard the night's report, she was in the intensive care unit. There had been no new admissions during the night so things were much as they had been the day before. Jade Jackson was looking a lot better this morning when she went to check on her. She was wide awake and Lucy could see that her skin was losing the distinctive yellow hue which had been caused by her jaundice.

A lot of babies developed mild jaundice in the days after their birth when their livers were unable to efficiently excrete bilirubin, the bile pigment which caused the discoloration. Jade's jaundice had been far more serious, though. She had been born with haemolytic disease, the result of her red blood cells being destroyed by antibodies produced by her mother while she was still in the womb due to rhesus incompatibility.

Fortunately, routine blood tests taken during the pregnancy had warned of the danger and Jade had been delivered four weeks early to minimise the risk of her becoming severely anaemic. Now Lucy smiled as she gently stroked the baby's cheek. This little patient would be on her way home before very long.

'Good morning, Staff.'

She felt her heart knock against her ribs as she recognised the familiar voice. She took a quick breath before she turned, determined to start as she meant to go on. Tom was a colleague now, nothing more, she reminded herself, yet as she saw him standing there looking so elegant in a well-cut charcoal-grey suit, she knew how difficult it was going to be remembering that.

'Good morning, sir,' she replied quietly, struggling to get a grip on herself. She glanced across the room while she tried to steady her nerves, but it didn't help when she saw Megan watching them with undisguised interest.

A little colour touched her cheeks as she quickly turned her back on the other woman and focused her attention firmly on work. 'I was just checking on baby Jackson. She was delivered four weeks early because of rhesus incompatibility and we're treating her for jaundice and anaemia.'

'She seems to be coming along nicely, from the look of her,' Tom observed, taking a long look at the baby before picking up her notes. 'I take it that she's having photo-therapy as well as the usual fluids to clear up the jaundice?'

He glanced at her for confirmation and Lucy nodded. 'Yes. Her bilirubin levels are dropping nicely, as you can see from the blood test results which came back yesterday. And her anaemia wasn't too serious, thanks to her being delivered early, so it doesn't pose a major problem.'

Tom nodded as he began reading carefully through all the notes, taking extra time to study the results of the previous day's blood tests. Lucy couldn't help smiling reminiscently as she watched him.

Tom had always been extremely thorough in everything he did, preferring to spend just that little bit extra time building up a complete picture of each patient to ensure that things were as they should be, and obviously he hadn't changed...

He suddenly looked up and she hurriedly smoothed her features into a suitably noncommittal expression, but she could tell by the slight frown he gave that she might not have been quick enough.

'That all seems to be fine to me, Staff. We'll continue her treatment and the blood tests but I'm not anticipating any major problems at this stage. When her parents come in, tell them how pleased we are with the way she's progressing, will you? I'm sure they must be worried.'

'Certainly, sir.' Lucy took the notes from him and popped them back into the holder at the bottom of the incubator, carefully avoiding his eyes. That was another thing about Tom she remembered: the consideration he had always shown to the relatives of his patients. All too often their needs were overlooked as many doctors seemed to think that it wasn't their job to worry about them. But not Tom.

Tom had always maintained that *everyone's* needs must be taken into account as far as possible and she knew how people had appreciated that. It seemed that he hadn't changed in that respect either and it was unsettling to realise it. It wasn't going to be easy to close the door on the past when there were these constant reminders to contend with.

'Apart from a general update on all the babies in the unit, I was particularly interested in seeing the Foster baby, Staff. Could you show me where she is?'

'Of course. She's over here.' Lucy pushed such disquieting thoughts to the back of her mind as she led the way across the room. Emma Foster, the baby's mother, was sitting by the incubator, staring at her daughter. The child was lying on her side and from this angle she looked absolutely perfect. It was only as they got closer that Lucy could see the bulge on her lower back where the malformed spinal cord was exposed.

Baby Abigail had been born with meningomyelocele, the severest form of spina bifida, and the outlook wasn't good. Even if she survived the next few days then there was little doubt that she would be severely handicapped. Lucy's heart went out to her mother as she laid a restraining hand on Emma's shoulder when she went to get up.

'No, stay there, Emma. Tom…Dr Farrell won't mind in the least if you stay while he examines Abigail.' She coloured at the unconscious slip although it was doubtful if Tom had noticed it. His attention was focused solely on the young mother, his face full of a deep compassion and concern.

'How are you bearing up, Mrs Foster?' he asked gently. 'This must be very hard for you.'

'It is,' Emma Foster admitted in a broken whisper. She raised a trembling hand to her face to wipe away a few tears as she looked at her baby. 'I know they said that she might have a problem but I just kept hoping, you see…'

She broke off as a sob welled from her lips. Tom gave her a moment to compose herself but Lucy could see that he was surprised by what he'd heard. 'So you knew beforehand that Abigail would have spina bifida, did you?' he prompted gently.

Emma nodded as she hunted in her dressing-gown pocket for a tissue. A lot of parents stayed in the hospital while their children were receiving treatment and the neo-natal intensive care unit had two self-contained suites for their use. Emma had opted to stay as she wanted to spend as much time as possible at her daughter's side. Lucy knew what a strain it must be for her as it was only a few days since she had given birth. Where the baby's father was she had no idea, because there had been no sign of him.

'Yes. Th…they told me at the hospital when I first went for a scan that there was something wrong. I…I didn't want to believe them,' Emma admitted in a choked voice.

'I imagine that you were offered a termination,' Tom said quietly. 'You and your husband chose not to have one, obviously.'

'He…he didn't know…about Abigail being…well, handicapped.' The words came out in a rush after that. 'I didn't tell Peter, you see, Doctor. I couldn't. I knew that he would want me to get rid of her and I just couldn't do it! So I didn't tell him what they'd said at the hospital. Now he's blaming me, says that it's all my fault and that I should never have had her!'

Emma began to sob wretchedly. Lucy hurriedly bent down and put her arm around her. 'Shh, it's all right, Emma. I'm sure once your husband has got over the initial shock that he'll understand why you couldn't bring yourself to tell him the truth.'

'He won't! He says that he won't ever forgive me and that he doesn't want to see me or Abigail ever again!'

Emma was inconsolable as she cried her heart out. Lucy looked over the top of her head and mouthed to Tom that she would take her back to her room. He nodded his agreement but, instead of leaving her to deal with the distraught woman, chose to help her. Slipping his hand under Emma's elbow, he gently urged her to her feet.

'Come along, Mrs Foster. You need to rest. You're not doing yourself any good wearing yourself out this way,' he said in a voice of such gentleness that Lucy felt a lump come to her throat.

'Is she going to die, Doctor?' Emma gulped back her tears for a second. There was such despair on her face that Lucy was hard pressed not to cry herself. 'I don't think I could bear it. I know she won't ever be the same as other children but I don't want her to die…!'

'I promise you that we shall do everything in our power to help your daughter.' Tom's voice was very firm and it obviously steadied the woman. He placed a guiding arm around Emma's shoulders as they led her back to her room. Lucy helped her into bed then glanced at Tom but he seemed to understand without her having to say anything.

'I think it would be a good idea if Mrs Foster had a mild sedative to help her sleep for a little while.' He turned to the wan-faced woman and smiled reassuringly. 'You have to rest, Mrs Foster. Abigail is going to need you in the coming weeks and you must try to build up your strength.

Giving birth is a tiring process for any woman but especially so when you are under the kind of strain you are having to cope with. I'll have Staff Nurse Benson bring you something to make you sleep for a couple of hours.'

'If you think I should. But you will fetch me if...if...?' Emma couldn't bring herself to voice her fears but they understood what she meant. Lucy patted her hand, wondering how the poor woman was going to cope if anything did happen to her baby.

'I'll come and get you if there is the slightest change in Abigail's condition. I promise,' she assured her softly.

'Thank you.' Emma turned onto her side and closed her eyes. She was crying softly as they left but the worst of the storm seemed to have passed.

Lucy closed the door quietly behind them and sighed. 'The poor thing! What must she be going through?'

'And without anyone at her side to support her, too!' Tom's tone was grim, his face set into harshly unforgiving lines when she glanced at him.

'I suppose it must have been a shock for her husband,' she suggested quietly, and heard him sigh.

'I imagine so. But just to turn his back on both of them... Hell! Which decent man would do a thing like that?' he declared hotly.

Lucy smiled sadly. 'I suspect there are a lot of men who would react that way in similar circumstances. And a lot of women as well who would find it impossible to deal with the thought of a handicapped child.'

'Maybe. However, you wouldn't be one of them, Lucy,' he stated emphatically. His grey eyes were very dark as they rested on her. She had no idea what he was thinking because it was impossible to read anything in their shimmering depths. It made it difficult to understand why she felt a *frisson* work its way down her spine, like the touch of a cool finger caressing her warm skin. There was nothing on Tom's face to cause it, nothing in the look he gave her— so steady and assured—and yet it happened all the same.

She took a quick breath, feeling strangely off balance so that it took a moment for his next words to sink in. 'You would cope with a situation like this, no matter how painful you found it. I always thought that you would make the perfect mother.'

Lucy felt the blood drain from her head as she realised what he had said. It took her all her time to remain standing as a wave of dizziness hit her. Tom took a quick step forward and grasped her arm as he saw how white she had gone.

'What is it? Lucy!'

She shrugged his hand off simply because she couldn't bear to feel those strong fingers clasping her cold flesh. It was too poignant to feel their strength and not be able to lean on it.

She had known how Tom had felt about her five years before, known that he'd been on the brink of asking her to marry him. That was why she had ended their relationship, although it had broken her heart to do so.

Until she'd met Tom she had given little conscious thought to the fact that she couldn't have children, although it had probably been a factor as to why she had never allowed anyone to get too close to her before.

Tom had been different, though. Before she had known what was happening she had been head over heels in love with him. However, when he had started talking about their future together, she had realised how impossible the situation was and that she had to end it.

She had loved him too much to deny him the family he had craved, yet she had known that if she had told him the truth he would have convinced her it didn't matter. It was the thought that at some point he might come to hate her which had given her the strength to make up the story that she had met someone else and was leaving Derbyshire to be with him. It had been the right thing to do, but to hear him say what he had just now was almost too painful. It took every scrap of control she possessed to pretend nothing was wrong.

'I...I'm fine. Really.' She gave him a tight smile, carefully avoiding his eyes in case she weakened even now. What was the point in raking up the past at this point? She would only embarrass him by making it seem as though she expected something from him.

'The only thing wrong with me is too little sleep,' she said lightly, latching onto the first thing which sprang to mind.

'I see. Out on the tiles last night, were you?' His tone was harsh all of a sudden, the look he gave her scathing, although she had no idea why. When he gave a deep laugh she actually jumped.

'Sorry, bit of a leading question, that, wasn't it? It's none of my business what you get up to.'

He turned away, walking swiftly to the office and going straight to the desk. Lucy followed him into the room, somewhat at a loss to know what was wrong. However, there was no hint of anything on his face as he wrote out a prescription for Emma Foster and handed it to her.

'Make sure she takes these, will you, please, Staff?' he instructed, glancing at his watch. 'I've a meeting with the rest of the team in ten minutes so I'll have to come back later. If you have any problems in the meantime, then page me.'

'Certainly, sir.'

She picked up the prescription and turned to leave, then paused as Tom said behind her, 'I think it would be easier if you and I tried to forget what happened in the past. I apologise for bringing it up just now. I was out of order.'

He shrugged as she glanced back, his face set into such remote lines that he looked like a stranger. 'It's always pointless looking back, I find. You can't undo the decisions you made, no matter how much you might want to do so.'

She wasn't sure what he meant. It had been her decision to end their relationship so he couldn't be referring to that.

She didn't say anything as she left the office, deeming it wiser to let the matter drop. However, the thought plagued her for a long time afterwards. What decision would Tom change if he could? It was only as she was going to the canteen for lunch that a possible answer hit her.

Had Tom meant that he would never have got involved with her if he could have done things all over again? The more she thought about it, the more likely it seemed, and her heart ached afresh as she realised that he regretted the time they had spent together. No wonder he had made it plain that he wanted to forget about the past!

'What we have to decide now is whether we operate. What do you say, Rob?'

Tom turned to his senior registrar, obviously keen to hear his views on baby Abigail's treatment. Lucy waited silently while Rob Turner took a moment to debate what he was going to say.

Tom had opted for an official ward round when he had come back from the team meeting and there was now a small crowd clustered around the incubator. Apart from Rob there was Meredith Gray, the junior house officer, plus two student doctors, one of whom was obviously shocked by his first sight of the baby.

St Elizabeth's had a strong teaching ethic and worked closely with the local school of medicine to provide students with experience in paediatric care. However, Lucy knew that it was quite different seeing at firsthand the effects of spina bifida from reading about it in a textbook, so she had a lot of sympathy for the young male student.

'I'm not sure if we should treat her,' Rob said thoughtfully. 'With this degree of spina bifida it's a foregone conclusion that she will be severely handicapped. There will be problems with motor, sensory, bladder and bowel functions, I would have thought.'

'I see. So what do you think, Meredith? Should we operate to close the spine and, hopefully, save her life? Or is the degree of handicap so severe that we would be simply condemning her to a life of suffering?' Tom asked, turning to the young woman.

Meredith bit her lip. She was a tall, slender girl with huge dark eyes and a gentle manner. Rumour had it that she and Rob were an item and Lucy hid a grin as she saw him give Meredith an encouraging smile.

Rob must have noticed she'd seen it because he winked at her. Lucy smiled back, not making any attempt to hide her amusement. She liked Rob because he had an easygoing manner which endeared him to everyone. They had been out together a couple of times in the past, to the cinema or for a drink. She had enjoyed his company mainly because there had been no strings attached to their friendship. Since Meredith had come on the scene, however, there had been little opportunity for them to see one another outside work, but she still considered him a friend and was glad that things were working out so well for him.

She was still smiling at that thought as she looked back at the incubator and happened to catch Tom's eye. She felt shock sear through her as she saw the expression on his face. What had she done to earn herself a look like that? she wondered, before quickly focusing her attention on what was going on.

'Well, I think I agree with Rob,' Meredith said hesitantly. 'One has to consider what her quality of life is going to be like.'

'And that is the only consideration?' Tom raised his brows as he looked round the group. He turned to Lucy. 'And what do you think, Staff? You must have your own views on what we should do?'

She was surprised to be consulted because it wasn't usual for the doctors to ask the nursing staff's opinion. Their last paediatric consultant had been extremely good but wouldn't have dreamt of asking her such a question. Now she took a moment to consider her answer, secretly pleased that Tom had had the courtesy to ask her opinion.

'Obviously, our main aim is to ensure that Abigail doesn't suffer in any way,' she said quietly. 'However, the parents' feelings must be taken into account in a case like this and any decisions which are made should be taken only when we are sure that they understand what repercussions it will have.'

'But nobody would want a child this badly handicapped!' the young student blurted out, immediately claiming everyone's attention. He looked uncomfortable as he realised what he had done.

It was always impressed upon the students that they should speak only when spoken to and most of the senior medical staff would have taken a very dim view of his outburst. Tom, however, didn't appear the least annoyed and once again Lucy was struck by his caring attitude. There was no question of him putting the younger doctor down for daring to state his views.

'You're right. A lot of people wouldn't want a severely handicapped child like this. However, in this case, the mother was aware of the problem throughout her pregnancy and chose to go ahead and have the baby,' he explained quietly. Lucy had noticed before that he never raised his voice and yet he seemed to command everyone's attention the moment he spoke. But then Tom had always had a certain presence about him which stemmed from confidence in his own ability. It had simply got stronger over the years and she felt a little surge of pride, which was quite ridiculous in the circumstances, of course.

'But does she fully understand all the implications?' Rob Turner frowned as he looked at Tom. 'I've seen children less severely handicapped than this child is going to be and I know how difficult it is for their parents to look after them and ensure any quality of life.'

'But do we have the right to deny the mother the opportunity if that is what she wants?' Meredith put in with sudden passion. 'I know we can make a decision based purely on medical grounds, but her feelings must be taken into account!'

It was the first time that Lucy had heard the other woman speak with such animation. She looked at her in surprise and happened to catch a glimpse of the expression on Tom's face. The best way to describe it was *satisfied* and she realised that he had set out to provoke just such a response from his team.

He must have sensed her looking at him because he glanced her way and smiled faintly, his brows arching meaningfully over amused grey eyes. Lucy smiled back, warmed by the way it made her feel to be included in his plans like this. The feeling stayed with her throughout the rest of the ward round, which turned out to be extremely lively and productive for everyone concerned. When she heard one of the students muttering that he'd learned more in the past hour then he'd learned in the last six months she knew that Tom had achieved his objective. His desire to pass on his knowledge was simply another indication of his dedication to the job and her admiration for him moved even further up the scale.

'There's coffee in the office for anyone who wants it,' she offered, struggling to get a grip on herself. It was hard enough dealing with this situation as it was, but to realise how much she still liked and admired Tom made it doubly difficult. All she could hope for was to put the intimacy of their past behind her and somehow learn to treat him as a respected colleague.

'Any biscuits, Lucy?' Rob Turner asked, laying a friendly arm around her shoulders. 'I missed breakfast this morning,' he explained soulfully, giving Meredith a meaningful look which brought an immediate rush of colour to the poor woman's cheeks.

Lucy hid her amusement. Rob was a terrible tease but it was obvious that he was smitten by Meredith and she by him. 'I might be able to find you some,' she replied, neatly sidestepping the friendly embrace.

'I'm afraid we shall have to pass on both coffee and biscuits.' Tom's tone was brisk yet she heard the undercurrent it held even if nobody else appeared to notice. She looked at him and was shocked to see a flash of anger in his eyes before he lowered his lids.

He didn't look at her again as he continued in the same no-nonsense tone. 'I want to get straight to Orthopaedics as there is a child there I want you all to see.'

He made his way to the lift, leaving the others no option but to follow him. Rob shrugged resignedly. He seemed to accept the situation at face value, as did Meredith and the students. Only Lucy had the feeling that Tom had made the decision not to break for coffee for some reason he wasn't admitting to...

She sighed as she pushed the thought firmly to the back of her mind. She was getting fanciful in her old age!

'Well, that's it. End of another shift.' Lucy finished changing into her outdoor clothes and glanced at Megan. 'Have you got anything planned while you're off for the next three days?'

'Decorating!' Megan sighed as she wriggled her way into a chunky hand-knitted sweater. 'I've nagged Jim into redoing the lounge so we'll be up to our eyes in paper and paste for the rest of the week.'

'No rest for the wicked, eh?' Lucy retorted with a sad lack of sympathy.

'Cheeky thing! I'll have you know that I don't have *time* to be wicked. Pure as the driven snow, that's me.' Megan grinned cheekily. 'We don't all have interesting pasts, Lucy Benson!'

Lucy knew what she meant and hastily opened the door to make her escape. 'Your trouble is that you have a vivid imagination. There is nothing at all interesting about my past, I assure you. Anyway, I'll love you and leave you. Good luck with the decorating.'

She whisked out of the door before Megan could say anything else, sighing as she swiftly made her way to the lifts. It was obvious that Megan was still curious about her and Tom and maybe it was her own fault. She should have admitted straight away that they had worked together. However, there was no point wishing she had done things differently because it wouldn't achieve anything. As Tom had said, it was impossible to wish decisions undone.

She groaned as she realised how obsessed she was becoming with the things he said. She would go home and have a long, hot soak in the bath, then cook herself a nice meal and spend the evening relaxing with a good book. And she wouldn't give Tom Farrell another thought!

She got out of the lift when it reached the ground floor but didn't immediately leave the building. St Elizabeth's had been built on the outskirts of Regent's Park and care had been taken to ensure that it fitted in with its surroundings. It was built from elegant grey brick in an L-shape, and the open space between the two arms had been glassed in to provide a covered entranceway and room for a mini shopping mall. Now she headed in that direction.

There were three shops in all: Dunwoody's, which sold fruit and flowers and also had a small but well-stocked grocery section; a post office selling stationery and a selection of paperback books and magazines; and a third shop called Foams which sold a range of toiletries and soft toys. She sniffed appreciatively as she went in through its door. After the clinical cleanliness of the intensive care unit it was wonderful to smell the delicious scent of apple blossom, even if it did come from a bottle!

She took her time selecting a small bottle of honeysuckle foam bath essence then took it to the counter. Miss Seddon, who ran the shop, popped it into one of the shop's distinctive gold-striped bags, smiling as she accepted the money. She was as immaculately dressed as always in a beautifully cut red suit, her dark hair caught back into an elegant coil, her make-up perfect.

Lucy was suddenly very conscious of her own lack of make-up and the fact that her hair needed washing and resolved to do something about both in the next few days. It was about time she made a little more effort with her appearance...

But for whose benefit? a small voice whispered silkily. Hers or Tom's?

She accepted her change and hurried out of the shop. Of course it hadn't anything to do with Tom Farrell! If she felt like smartening herself up, then it was for her own sake. However, it was harder to shake off the thought than it should have been. It kept nagging away as she paid old Mr Goode for the paperback novel she had selected and kept her company as she went to Dunwoody's to buy something for her tea.

Lucy responded as best she could as Mrs Lewis, the middle-aged lady who ran the shop, chatted away but she couldn't remember a word of what had been said a few moments later. All that kept coming to mind was that same silly thought—that she wanted Tom to still find her attractive!

She headed for the exit at a brisk pace, suddenly anxious to put as much distance as she could between herself and the possibility of running into Tom again that day. If she had time to adjust to the situation then she could get things into perspective, she reasoned. After all, it *had* been a shock to discover they would be working together and she really *hadn't* had time to adapt to it. However, with the benefit of three days off, things would appear far less complicated.

She let out a sigh of relief as she realised there was an easy answer to her predicament. She had reached the doors by then and was just about to open the one nearest to her when a hand reached past her and opened it for her. Even though she could see nothing but the hand plus a few inches of crisp white shirt-cuff, she knew who it belonged to. It wasn't a surprise when a familiar voice said, 'Allow me,' so she couldn't blame that for the *frisson* which raced down her spine. And there was no excuse at all for the way her heart began to pound as she looked round and saw Tom behind her. It was all down to her, to the way she felt, to the way Tom *made* her feel even now. In the circumstances it wasn't the most comforting of thoughts.

How could she hope to put things into perspective when being around Tom made her wish for all sorts of crazy things which could never happen?

CHAPTER THREE

'ON YOUR way home?'

'Er…yes.' Funny how difficult it was to reply to such a simple question. Lucy hurried out of the door, struggling to get a grip on herself. So much for all her assurances that she could learn to deal with this situation when all it took was Tom's sudden appearance to send her into a spin!

He paused to hold the door open for a woman coming out behind them and she took the opportunity to set off down the path at a brisk pace. The last thing she wanted was for Tom to think that she expected him to accompany her. However, he soon caught her up, his long legs making short work of the start she had on him.

'You seem in a hurry,' he observed, glancing sideways at her from under frowning black brows. 'Got something planned for tonight—a hot date, perhaps?'

'Hardly!' She gave a dismissive laugh as she carried on walking. It was gone five and the January night had already grown dark. There was a sharp easterly wind blowing which cut through her quilted jacket. She turned her collar up, wondering how Tom could stand to be outside wearing only a suit. He didn't appear to notice the cold, however, as he strode along beside her, one hand tucked casually into the pocket of his trousers, his jacket flapping open.

Lucy felt a little shiver dance down her spine as she saw how the wind had plastered his white shirt against the lean muscles of his chest. She looked away at once, uncomfortable with how it made her feel. So Tom *was* an attractive man, but did that explain the way she responded to him? Or did it owe itself to something more, perhaps—to some echo of what she had felt for him five years before?

'Why so surprised? I'm sure you must have your fair share of dates, Lucy? Are you seeing anyone at the moment? Or is that the sort of question I shouldn't be asking?' He shrugged as she glanced at him. 'I know we agreed not to talk about the past but I can't help being curious about what's happened to you.'

'Not a lot,' she replied shortly. 'My life has been fairly uneventful so far, I assure you.'

'So there's no one special in your life at present, then?' He gave a deeply sardonic laugh. 'I hope Rob knows that. I wouldn't like him to be in for a nasty shock, too.'

'Rob?' she queried blankly, feeling slightly sick as she heard the mockery in his voice. Had Tom been referring to the shock he'd had when she had told him that she had met someone else and was leaving Derbyshire? she wondered, then immediately dismissed the idea.

It had happened too long ago to still bother him, and too much had happened in his life since, like his marriage and Adam's arrival in the world. However, that didn't explain what he had meant.

'I'm not sure what you are getting at, Tom,' she stated flatly. 'And I certainly don't know anyone called Rob...' She gasped as she came to an abrupt halt. Her brown eyes were enormous as she stared at him. 'You don't mean Rob Turner, do you?'

He looked momentarily uncomfortable, as though her surprise had surprised him. 'I got the impression that you and he were...' He paused uncertainly, but Lucy could feel the first stirrings of anger so carried on for him in a taut little voice which told of her displeasure.

'That we were what? Friends? Colleagues? Because that's all Rob and I are, I can assure you!'

She started walking again, her feet flying along the tarmacadamed surface. She wasn't sure why she was so annoyed. So what if Tom had made a genuine mistake by thinking there had been more to Rob Turner's friendly hug? If anyone else had suggested it, she would have laughed out loud, and yet she felt deeply hurt that Tom should have imagined anything was going on.

'Mmm, seems I got that all wrong, doesn't it?'

There was a wry note in his voice which gained her immediate attention and she shot him a wary look. He gave her a crooked grin. 'Sorry, Lucy. I think it was rather a case of adding two and two and coming up with five thousand!'

She couldn't help smiling at the rueful comment. 'Well, maths was never your strong point, was it, Tom?'

He groaned exaggeratedly. 'Oh, that was below the belt! Just because I once made a teeny little slip…'

'Teeny?' Hands on shapely hips, Lucy rounded on him. 'All I asked you to do was check that my adding up was correct when I'd been working out how much money I had left in my bank account. And what did you do, only "discover" that I had fifty pounds more than I thought I had!'

'So you went straight out and blew it on a new dress for the party we were going to that night,' he put in with a deep chuckle.

Lucy glowered, although it was hard not to laugh when she thought back to what had happened. 'Yes! And then had to eat jam sandwiches for the rest of the month until I got paid because I had no more housekeeping money!'

'It was worth it, though. I remember how gorgeous you looked when we went out that night. Every guy at that party envied me.'

He smiled reminiscently, mercifully missing her shocked gasp as she heard what he said. It took her all her time to concentrate as he continued in the same pensive tone.

'I did offer to lend you some money, if you remember, but you were so independent that you refused. You really should have accepted it, Lucy.'

'No way!' She shook her head, struggling to control the mixture of emotions she felt at that moment. Tom's comment about how she had looked had touched a nerve and it was hard to dismiss it. Maybe that was what caused her to lower her guard.

'I knew very well that if I accepted it you would refuse to let me pay you back. You were always so generous, Tom. It was one of the things I lo…'

She broke off in horror as she realised what she had been about to say, that it had been one of the things she'd loved most about him. Tom took a deep breath as he looked up at the sky.

'One of the things you liked about me? But obviously *liking* wasn't enough, was it? You met someone else and that was it.' He looked back at her and she had to steel herself to meet his gaze without flinching.

'What happened between you and the chap you left me for, Lucy? I suppose it's another question I shouldn't ask but you can't blame me for wanting to know. When you left Derbyshire I thought that you were planning on getting married, but I can't see any sign of a ring.'

She turned away, feeling sick to her stomach at having to give credence to the lie she had told him five years before. 'It just didn't work out, that's all,' she stated flatly.

'I'm sorry. It's always upsetting when a relationship doesn't come up to expectations.'

He sounded so cold and clinical that she couldn't help shivering. He must have noticed because he started walking again, setting a brisk pace as they left the hospital grounds and headed along the road. Traffic was heavy with the rush hour under way and they had to wait for the lights to change before they could safely cross over to the other side.

Lucy paused when they reached the opposite pavement, not sure what to do. She certainly didn't want to prolong the meeting yet she was reluctant just to walk off. Tom must have such a poor opinion of her because of the way she had treated him and it hurt to know that. Yet what could she say to make things better apart from the truth, and she'd already decided it was too late for that?

'Well, I'd better go or I'll miss my bus,' she said quickly

before the desire to make amends overruled common sense. 'You must be anxious to get home and see Adam with it being his first day with his new nanny, I expect. I assume that's why you brought him to work with you yesterday, because she wasn't there to look after him?'

'She started last week, actually. I took Adam with me yesterday so that he would have an idea where I am when I can't be with him.' Tom shrugged but Lucy saw the pain which darkened his eyes. 'He gets very upset when I have to leave him. He's afraid that I won't come back. I thought it might help to reassure him if he saw where I worked.'

'Oh, what a shame! I suppose it must have something to do with him missing his mother? He probably can't understand why she has disappeared from his life?' Lucy suggested, her heart aching at the thought of the little boy's confusion.

'Probably.' There was a shade less conviction in Tom's voice than there might have been and she looked at him curiously. However, if he noticed, he obviously chose not to enlighten her as to its cause. He cast an expressive glance at the dark sky instead and shuddered.

'Right, I'll get on home, then. I only live in those flats over there, thankfully enough. If I had to go much further I'd probably turn into a walking iceberg. It's absolutely freezing out tonight!'

Lucy laughed dutifully as she glanced at the expensive block of flats further along the road but she couldn't hide her curiosity. 'Is that why you came out without a coat today, because you don't have far to walk to work?'

He gave a rather self-conscious grimace. 'Not exactly. I left my coat in my office. I was in…in a bit of a rush and forgot about it.'

He gave her a last quick smile then hurried away. He didn't pause to look back as he turned into the forecourt of the flats, but why should he? It had been pure coincidence that they had happened to meet up as they were both leaving work. To imagine anything else was ridiculous. Yet, no matter how illogical it sounded, she couldn't shake off the feeling that Tom had seen her leaving and come rushing after her…

She sighed as she began walking swiftly towards the bus stop. Oh, yes, and pigs might fly!

Lucy was enjoying a second cup of tea the next morning when the phone rang. Surprisingly, she had slept well. Obviously, the long soak in the bath followed by a few pleasant hours spent reading her new novel had worked wonders, because her sleep hadn't been interrupted by any of the dreams which had plagued her the night before.

Maybe she was getting used to the idea of Tom being back in her life, she mused as she hurried into the hall and picked up the receiver. And perhaps running into him like that on her way home hadn't been such a disaster? Apart from a few terse seconds they had managed to talk to one another like—well, like two old friends, so her hopes were high that they could work things out. However, all it took was the sound of Tom's voice to set her right back to square one. Which other old friend managed to make her pulse race this way?

'I'm sorry to ring you at this time of the day, Lucy, but I'm at my wits' end.' Tom wasted no time as he got down to the reason why he was calling her. 'I need to ask you a huge favour. I know you're off duty today so could you possibly look after Adam for a few hours?'

Lucy blinked because it was the last thing she'd expected him to say. 'Well…yes, of course I will. But what's happened to his nanny?'

'Gone.' Tom's tone was grim. Lucy could hear the anger it held and felt her stomach sink. One read such awful things in the newspapers…

'Is Adam all right?' she demanded urgently. 'He isn't hurt?'

'No, thank heavens. He's just upset and very confused.' He sighed heavily. 'Look, I'll explain everything properly when you get here. Would you come as soon as you can? I know it's a huge imposition to ask…'

'Don't worry about it, Tom. I'm only too happy to help, really. Just tell me the number of your flat and I'll be there as fast as I can.'

She jotted down the number then, brushing aside his thanks, hung up. Hurrying into her bedroom, she quickly dressed in jeans and a warm toffee-coloured chenille sweater which she had bought on her last pay day. A slick of lip gloss and a little mascara were all she had time for by the way of make-up, then she quickly ran a brush through her hair, thanking heaven that she had washed it the previous night so that it fell silkily around her face.

Considering the amount of time she'd had, she didn't look *too* bad, she decided critically, taking a last look at her reflection…

She turned away in sudden impatience. What did it matter how she looked? It was doubtful if Tom would notice, nor did she want him to. The days when she had dressed up for Tom Farrell's benefit were long gone!

It took her almost thirty minutes to get to the flat. Tom opened the door as soon as she rang the bell, smiling in relief when he saw her. 'Lucy, thank you! I can't tell you how grateful I am for this. Here, let me take your coat.'

He helped her off with her jacket and hung it on a peg then turned back to her. His grey eyes made a lightning-fast assessment of what she was wearing before he smiled. 'Mmm, a definite improvement on the uniform. That sweater is lovely on you, really brings out the colour of your eyes.'

'I…er…thank you.' She could feel the hot rush of colour which swept up her face at the compliment and quickly changed the subject. 'Where's Adam?'

'He's still asleep. He's worn out, poor little chap. I ended up taking him into bed with me but it was ages before he settled down so I won't wake him up just yet.' Tom's tone was grim as he nodded towards a partly open door on the far side of the hall. Lucy caught a glimpse of a small form huddled beneath a brightly patterned quilt before Tom touched her arm, indicating that she should follow him.

He led the way into the kitchen and went straight to the kettle and switched it on. 'Tea?'

'Yes, but only if you're having some. If you want to get off, Tom…' she began, but he shook his head.

'I would prefer to wait until Adam wakes up. The poor kid has been through quite enough in the past twelve hours.'

His face was set into such grim lines that she shivered. She drew a chair out from the small pine table and sat down. 'What's been happening, Tom? Obviously, there has been some sort of an upset or you wouldn't have phoned me.'

'I wouldn't have phoned anyone else in the circumstances, Lucy. There isn't anyone I would trust Adam with apart from you.'

There was no doubting he meant it and she felt a warm little glow settle in her heart. She looked down at the table so that he wouldn't see how touched she was by the admission. 'Thank you. I appreciate that.'

'It's no more than the truth.' He turned away as the kettle came to the boil, swiftly making two mugs of tea which he brought back to the table. He handed her one of them and sat down.

'It's been one hell of a night, one way or the other. I'm still trying to get to grips with what happened, to tell the truth.'

'Tell me about it,' she encouraged, taking a sip of the hot tea.

He took a deep breath before he began in a deliberately flat tone. 'I'd only been home about an hour when the hospital phoned to say that I might be needed. There'd been a car crash on the outskirts of the city and one of the vehicles involved was being driven by a woman who was thirty weeks pregnant. The fire brigade had started to cut her out of the wreckage but she'd gone into labour and there were grave concerns for the baby with it being so premature.'

'How dreadful!' Lucy exclaimed. 'It must have been a nightmare for everyone concerned.'

'So I imagine. There were several fatalities, it appears, but obviously my main concern was the baby. I knew that I could be called out at any moment so I explained to Tracey, Adam's nanny, that she would have to stay in.'

'And there was a problem about that?' Lucy suggested quietly.

'How did you guess?' Tom sighed as he tipped his chair back and stared at the ceiling. Lucy could see how tired he looked. There were dark circles under his eyes and lines either side of his mouth. Her heart went out to him as she realised how difficult it must be balancing work and looking after Adam.

He let the chair snap back onto all four legs and picked up his cup. 'I could tell Tracey wasn't pleased but I never gave it much thought. I was more concerned about the problems I would face when I got to the hospital. I'd been told that they would bring the baby in by helicopter so I knew that it wouldn't take long.'

He paused to sip his tea. 'Anyway, it was just before seven when I received a call to say the helicopter was on its way so I went straight over there. The baby was in a pretty bad way, what with the shock of the accident and being so premature. We worked on her for a couple of hours and finally managed to get her stable. I decided to pop back here to check on Adam and then go back to the hospital in case there was anything else I could do.'

He stopped and she saw him take a deep breath, as though the next part of the tale was almost too painful to relate. Without stopping to think, she reached across the table and squeezed his hand.

'What happened when you got back here, Tom?'

He stared at her blankly for a moment, then suddenly thrust back his chair. Walking to the window, he stood with his back to her, but she could tell how upset he was from the clipped tone of his voice.

'As soon as I opened the front door I knew something was wrong. Adam was screaming his head off; he sounded completely hysterical, in fact. I ran straight to his room and he was just sitting up in bed, rigid with terror. I picked him up and went to find Tracey but there was no sign of her. Evidently, she had decided that there was no way she was forgoing her evening's entertainment and gone out, leaving Adam by himself.'

'No! But that's awful. He must have been so scared, waking up and finding nobody here.' She couldn't hide her dismay and she saw Tom's face pale as he looked round.

'I know! I can't stop thinking about how terrified he must have been, especially after...' He stopped abruptly, shaking his head as though to clear it of some dreadful memory. Lucy found herself wondering what it could be but there was no way she could ask him at that moment.

She concentrated instead on what had gone on the night before. 'So what happened after that? Did Tracey come back?'

'Oh, yes. About five minutes after I got here. I expect she thought that she'd have plenty of time to sneak out without me knowing. What haunts me is the fact that I *wouldn't* have known if I hadn't come back to check on Adam. I was in two minds whether or not I should do so, in fact.'

He gave a sardonic laugh but she could hear the pain it held and knew that he blamed himself for what had happened. 'I was worried in case she thought that I didn't trust her, would you believe?'

'But you did come back, Tom, and that's what you have to think about. I know Adam must have been scared but children are resilient. He will get over it in time,' she assured him, hating to see him berating himself for something which hadn't been his fault.

'I hope so,' he said grimly, then suddenly sighed. 'Anyway, in a nutshell, I told Tracey to pack her bags. I ordered a taxi and sent her to a hotel for the night. First thing this morning I got onto the agency who sent her to me and told them exactly what had happened.

'They were most apologetic and promised to look into it, but it still leaves me with the problem of what to do. It could be days before I find someone to replace her, and that's assuming I can bring myself to trust anyone to look after Adam ever again after this!'

'I'm sure you were just unfortunate this time,' Lucy assured him, mentally crossing her fingers. How would she feel if it had been her child? she wondered, already knowing the answer. She would have found it very hard to leave her child with anyone ever again after a scare like that. It made her realise what a huge compliment Tom had paid her by putting his trust in her.

There was a catch in her voice as she hurried to reassure him. 'Anyway, I'm here now and Adam will be absolutely fine with me, Tom. I promise you that.'

'I know he will. You are the one person I *can* trust to look after him, Lucy. I know that he couldn't be in safer hands. It's just such a huge imposition putting on you like this.' He grimaced and she could see the uncertainty in his eyes. 'I think I'm just realising how huge, in fact!'

'Rubbish! What are friends for if not to help one another in times like this?' she declared, then felt her heart beat a little faster as he gave her a searching look.

'I hope we can be friends again, Lucy. I know I would like that more than anything,' he stated quietly.

She looked away, hoping that he couldn't guess how that made her feel. Of course she wanted to be friends with Tom and she was glad that he felt it was possible after what had happened in the past. Yet a tiny inner voice was whispering that she would like to be more than just his friend if she had the choice. It scared her because it was pointless thinking like that. The time for her and Tom to make any kind of commitment other than friendship was long past.

She realised that he expected her to say something so summoned a smile. 'Me, too. I…I always valued our friendship, Tom.'

He inclined his head gravely, although there was a glitter of something hot and a little bit wild in his eyes… She closed her mind to what it meant and was glad that she had when he continued in a brisk, no-nonsense tone which told her that her imagination might have been playing tricks.

'Right, then I'd better fill you in on Adam's routine. He isn't difficult to deal with normally, but he may still be upset by what went on last night so he could be a little bit fractious,' he warned.

'I realise that.' Lucy smiled understandingly. 'I expect I'd be upset in his shoes, poor little mite!'

'Sorry. I'm rather stating the obvious, aren't I? I don't mean to sound like a fussing father!' he declared with a grimace.

'You sound like a very *caring* father, Tom. But then I wouldn't have expected anything else.' Her brown eyes were warm as they met his. 'You never made any secret of how much you wanted children. Having a family meant more to you than anything else, I always thought.'

'Did you?' He gave her an oddly intent look. Lucy wasn't sure what was behind it, and before she could work it out he carried on. 'Anyway, to get back to Adam, can you possibly stay until this afternoon? I'll try to get back as soon as I can, but I'm due in theatre so I'll be tied up for most of the morning. Then there is last night's admission…'

'It's fine, Tom. Really. I can stay as long as you need me to.' She could tell that he still wasn't convinced and smiled. 'I hadn't anything planned apart from catching up on housework and that can easily wait, believe me!'

'Well, if you're sure—' he began, then broke off as there was a tearful wail of 'Daddy' from the bedroom. He hurried out of the room and came back a few seconds later with Adam clinging around his neck.

'Look who's here to see you, tiger,' he said softly, turning so that the little boy could see her. 'You remember Lucy, don't you? Say hello.'

Adam stared at her for a moment, then quickly buried his face in Tom's neck. Lucy shook her head when it looked as though Tom was going to try to cajole the child into speaking to her. Deliberately ignoring him, she went to the fridge and took out a bottle of apple juice, then found a bright red plastic beaker in the cupboard and poured some juice into it.

Adam shifted slightly, peeping at her from under his lashes as he watched what she was doing, although he was careful to retain a tight hold on Tom. His solemn expression was a mirror image of his father's as he watched while she found a packet of cereal in the cupboard and poured some into a bowl, then fetched a fresh bottle of milk from the fridge. However, the popping of the puffed rice as the milk was poured over it worked like magic.

'Down, Daddy,' he ordered imperiously, but Tom gave him a level look.

'What's the magic word?' he asked firmly, and Lucy was glad that he hadn't fallen into the trap of letting Adam get away with forgetting what he had been taught. The best way to see the child through this episode was to behave as normally as possible, in her view, and Tom obviously agreed.

'Please. Please can Adam get down?' the little boy repeated, looking longingly at the bowl of cereal.

'Of course you can. Good boy.' Tom put him down, watching with a mixture of relief and concern as the child scrambled onto a chair and began hungrily tucking into his breakfast.

'He'll be fine, Tom. You'll see.'

Lucy touched him lightly on the arm, wanting to offer some comfort for what he was going through. He turned to smile at her and it seemed as though a weight had been lifted off his shoulders all of a sudden.

'I think you're right. Thank you, Lucy. I can't tell you how grateful I am that you came.'

She gave him a quick smile then moved away to gather up their cups to wash them. Being witness to the depth of love that Tom felt for his son was deeply moving, but it was only to be expected. Adam was all he had left of his dead wife so he must be doubly precious because of that.

Her heart ached sharply at the thought of the woman who had shared Tom's life in recent years. She knew it was wrong to feel so envious in the circumstances, but she couldn't help it. Fiona had given Tom the one thing she could never have given him and, right or wrong, she envied her that!

'Lucy have some juice, too?'

Adam suddenly claimed her attention and she made a determined effort to put such negative thoughts out of her head. Going over to the table, she bent down and pretended to drink some of the juice from the beaker when he solemnly offered it to her.

'Mmm, that was delicious! Thank you, sweetie.'

'You're welcome,' he replied, sounding so grown up that it was hard not to laugh. She glanced at Tom in amusement and was stunned to see the look of regret on his face. However, it disappeared so fast as he gave her a conspiratorial wink that she decided her imagination had been playing tricks again.

'What did I say about three going on ninety-three?' he asked softly and she laughed.

By the time Adam had finished his breakfast he seemed a lot happier. Tom took him on his knee and quietly explained that, as he had to go to work, Lucy was going to look after him. She guessed that he was holding his breath as Adam gave her a long, considering look. However, in the end the little boy nodded, although he looked momentarily unsure when Tom went to get changed.

Seeing the child's lower lip beginning to quiver ominously, she decided that diversionary tactics were called for. She placed one of the kitchen chairs by the sink, then rolled up the sleeves of Adam's pyjamas and stood him on it.

'Let's wash these dishes,' she suggested, adding an extravagantly large squirt of washing-up liquid to the warm water. She frothed up the soapsuds then bent and whispered in his ear, 'And then I can teach you how to blow bubbles, if you want me to.'

Adam's eyes lit up at the prospect. He forgot all about his father leaving him alone. By the time Tom came back, suave as ever in a navy suit and pale blue shirt, there were rainbow-hued bubbles floating all round the kitchen.

'Look, Daddy. Watch me!' Adam sucked in a huge breath and blew a massive bubble, then gasped as it exploded in his face. He appeared momentarily shocked before he broke into peals of delighted laughter. Lucy hugged him tight as she lifted him down from the chair and dried his hands on a towel.

'That was the biggest bubble I've ever seen! Now give Daddy a kiss before he goes to work. Then we can go to the park and play on the swings, if you want to?'

'Yes!' Adam raced across the kitchen and plonked a perfunctory kiss on Tom's cheek. 'Bye, Daddy.' He turned excitedly to Lucy. 'Go now?'

'Just as soon as you're washed and dressed, young man,' she assured him, laughing as he raced off towards the bathroom.

'I don't think I need worry about him, from the look of it,' Tom said softly. 'It seems you've worked your magic on him, Lucy, although I don't know why I should be surprised.'

There was a nuance in his voice which brought her gaze to his face and she coloured as she saw the warmth in his grey eyes. Her heart seemed to be beating in short, sharp bursts so that she felt suddenly breathless and dizzy, a feeling which intensified as he continued in the same warmly melodious tone.

'Adam isn't the first Farrell to fall under your spell.'

He didn't say anything more before he left. Maybe he realised that it would be wrong to do so. After all, they had agreed to be friends and there was a limit to what that meant. Overstepping the boundaries was something neither of them wanted...did they?

CHAPTER FOUR

IT WAS almost three before Tom got back. Lucy got up as soon as she heard the front door opening, putting a finger to her lips as she went out to the hall to meet him.

'Shh. Adam's having a nap so don't wake him up,' she warned in a whisper.

Tom's brows rose steeply as he shrugged off his overcoat. 'He doesn't usually have a sleep in the afternoon nowadays.'

'He was exhausted, poor little love.' She tiptoed back to the lounge, smiling as she looked at the small figure curled up on the sofa. 'I was reading to him after lunch and, the next thing I knew, he was fast asleep.'

'It will do him the world of good, I expect. But then having this morning with you, Lucy, has already worked wonders for him, I can tell.'

Tom's voice was soft in keeping with the need not to wake the child, yet there was a note in it which made a shiver work its way down her spine. She gave him a quick smile then hurriedly led the way to the kitchen, afraid that she might be reading too much into it. Obviously, Tom was grateful for her help and pleased that Adam was all right, but…

But nothing! that pesky little voice piped up as it had kept on doing lately. Tom had meant what he'd said…without reservations!

'Would you like something to eat?' she offered hastily, trying to close her mind to such disturbing thoughts. 'Adam and I had fish fingers and beans for lunch because he said it was his favourite. I hope that was all right.'

Tom laughed as he sat at the table. 'Fine, and he wasn't

kidding when he said it was his favourite meal. He would have it every day of the week if he could. Hopefully, he will have developed a more sophisticated palate by the time he's twenty!'

Lucy chuckled at that. 'I shouldn't worry too much. My niece, Jessica, went through a spell like that when she was Adam's age. She would only eat cheese and Marmite sandwiches for breakfast, lunch and tea! I can remember my poor sister, Cathy, trying everything she could think of to tempt her to eat something else, but she wouldn't be budged. However, Jessica eats everything you put in front of her now, so I'm sure Adam is just going through a similar phase.'

'I expect you're right. Anyway, I would love a sandwich if you don't mind, Lucy. I didn't stop for lunch so that I could get back here as soon as I could.'

She plugged in the kettle then hastened to reassure him, realising how worried he must have been. 'Adam has been fine, honestly, Tom. We went to the park after you left and played on the swings. Then, when we got back, I made him some play-dough out of some flour and salt and a bit of food colouring I found at the back of the cupboard.'

She smiled as she picked up a tray and showed him the misshapen figures the child had made out of the bright pink dough. 'He insisted on keeping them to show you. I think you may have a budding Henry Moore on your hands. He seems to have a real talent for sculpting, from the look of these!'

Tom laughed as he studied the pink blobs. 'Obviously, Adam's work veers towards the abstract, wouldn't you say?'

'Oh, undoubtedly!' she agreed, laughing as she put the tray back on the counter.

'You're a miracle worker, Lucy; do you know that? When I think back to the state he was in last night!'

His voice was gruff, making her realise just how worried he had been. When she turned to look at him he smiled at her with such relief that she was in little doubt that he meant every word. 'Thank you for what you've done this morning. Oh, I don't just mean for coming over here to look after Adam, although I really am grateful for that, believe me. But what I appreciate more than anything is the way you've helped him get over the fright he had last night.'

He reached out and captured her hand. 'I don't know how I can ever repay you.'

Lucy felt her heartbeat accelerate until it felt as though it were going to beat its way right out of her chest. The warmth in Tom's voice, not to mention the touch of his hand, was setting up a chain of reactions.

She took a deep breath as she drew her hand away, afraid that the temptation to let it remain might overrule common sense. Tom was grateful for her help but that was all there was to it. To imagine anything else would be foolish.

'Do…don't be silly. I'm only too glad to help. Now, how about beef and salad in that sandwich? I noticed there was some in the fridge.'

She quickly set about making the sandwich and a pot of coffee so that he wouldn't guess how she felt, so on edge and keyed up that every nerve in her body seemed to be jumping. It was an effort to appear natural as she put the plate in front of him.

'Eat up,' she ordered sternly. 'I don't suppose you had any breakfast, either, so you must be starving.'

'I am.' His stomach chose that precise moment to rumble loudly and they both laughed. It helped dispel some of the tension so that it was easier to behave naturally as she poured him a cup of coffee.

'Aren't you having one?' he asked in surprise when he saw there was only one cup.

'Well…' She hesitated, unsure whether it was wise to stay any longer when just these few minutes in Tom's company had caused such havoc.

'Just a quick cup of coffee to keep me company while I

eat,' he said persuasively. He gave her a soulful look, although the note in his voice was only partly teasing. 'Nothing spoils a meal more than not having anyone to share it with.'

'Mmm, I don't know if a few sandwiches can be classed as a meal,' she retorted, determinedly keeping the tone light. 'It's hardly haute cuisine, placing cold meat and salad between two slices of bread!'

'It depends on what you're used to.' He took an appreciative bite then rolled his eyes in exaggerated pleasure as he chewed it.

Lucy laughed as she filled a second cup with coffee and sat down. 'OK, I'll stay and have a cup of coffee. You don't have to go overboard with the compliments!'

Tom wiped his mouth on a piece of kitchen roll, which was all she had been able to find to serve as a napkin. 'It wasn't an exaggeration. Meals in this house tend to be nursery fare, i.e. fish fingers and beans, sausages and mash, that sort of thing. To actually eat something grown-up like a beef sandwich with *mustard* is a real treat!'

She laughed at that but she couldn't help thinking how hard it must be for him, bringing up a small child on his own. 'I suppose it's easier if you cook something Adam likes rather than make two separate meals?'

'Uh-huh.' He finished the last morsel of sandwich and sat back in his chair with a sigh of contentment. 'To be honest I find it hard to fit everything in. There just don't seem to be enough hours in a day.'

'It must be hard,' she sympathised. 'There are all the practical things to be done like washing and shopping, aren't there? But if you're not careful they can take up every spare minute so that you don't have any time to spend with Adam, and that's so important.'

'Exactly. I feel guilty enough about the amount of time I have to spend away from him without wasting even more time when I'm at home cooking elaborate meals,' Tom agreed regretfully.

'Maybe you should think of hiring a housekeeper?' Lucy suggested thoughtfully. 'Then any free time you have could be solely devoted to Adam.'

'It would be great if I could do that but I'm afraid finances don't allow for that sort of a luxury.' Tom shrugged. 'I can just about manage to cover the cost of a nanny as it is.'

Lucy frowned. 'Really? But surely now that you've got this consultancy—?' She stopped abruptly, realising how rude it was to question him about his finances. However, Tom didn't appear annoyed. He gave a deep sigh as he finished what she'd been going to say.

'Now that I've been made a consultant I should be able to afford all the help I need?' He shook his head. 'I'm afraid not. It just isn't that simple.'

He didn't add anything more, leaving her wondering what on earth he had meant about it not being simple. However, there was no way she could ask him such a personal question so she quickly turned the conversation to what must be uppermost on his mind at that moment.

'Did you manage to get in touch with the agency again about the new nanny?'

'Yes. I spoke to the manager before I left work. However, she wasn't much help. It appears that most of their girls expect to work set hours and, like Tracey, would take a dim view of having to change their plans at the last minute if I were called out unexpectedly of an evening.'

'But that's ridiculous! Surely you explained that you would be called into work only if it was an emergency,' Lucy exclaimed.

'I did but it cut no ice. Anyway, I left it with her and phoned round a couple of other agencies as well, so I'll just have to wait and see what happens.' He laughed ruefully. 'And to think that one of the main attractions of moving to London was that I would be spared this problem!'

She laughed with him, although she knew how concerned he must be about finding adequate child care. 'I'm sure someone suitable will turn up, Tom. What are you going to do in the meantime, though? Didn't you once mention that your mother lived fairly close to London, so would she help out?'

'Like a shot if she were here, but she's gone to New Zealand for six months to visit my sisters. They both live there now and Susie has just had a baby so Mum was dying to see her.' He ran his hand through his hair and sighed. 'I don't want her finding out about the problems I'm having or she will be on the next plane back, knowing her!'

'I see. Well, if it would help, I could look after Adam for the next couple of days while I'm off duty?' she offered, but he immediately shook his head.

'No, I can't let you do that. You've done enough already.'

'I don't mind!' she assured him. 'To tell the truth I've enjoyed today. I always love being with children and Adam is a such a little poppet. I really miss my niece Jessica now that I live so far away from her,' she added wistfully.

'I'm sure you do. But then the best thing about other people's children is that you can hand them back at the end of the day, isn't it, Lucy?'

There was a nuance in his voice as he said that which she didn't understand, but before she had time to think about it he continued. 'Anyway, much as I appreciate your offer, there is no need for me to take up any more of your time than I already have. I've made arrangements for Adam to go to the hospital crèche for the next couple of weeks. Amanda Grayson suggested it when I was called down to Outpatients this morning and happened to mention that I was having problems. Evidently, it has a very good reputation among the staff. I popped in before I came home, and, as luck would have it, they have a temporary vacancy while one of the children is on holiday for a couple of weeks. Hopefully, I'll have found another nanny by then.'

'Well, so long as you're sure…' she began.

'I am. It's better this way, believe me.' He stared down

at his coffee, then lifted his head and looked her straight in the eyes. 'I'm really grateful for what you've done today, Lucy, but I don't want Adam getting too attached to you. It will only confuse him even more and he's had enough upsets in his young life as it is.'

'Surely the same applies to any nanny he has,' she countered, wondering why she was arguing the point when it was obvious that Tom had made up his mind. It was just that his flat refusal of her help had touched a nerve.

He shook his head impatiently. 'It isn't the same! Oh, I know Adam might grow fond of a nanny, assuming I ever find one who will stay long enough, of course! But it's an entirely different situation letting him become attached to you.'

He shrugged but she could see the determination in his eyes. 'At the end of the day Adam isn't your responsibility. You have your own life to lead and I can't imagine that you want to clutter it up with looking after someone else's child.'

It was obvious that he wasn't going to be swayed by anything she said and maybe he was right. It would be unfair to let Adam grow fond of her when she could never play a real role in his life.

The thought was more painful than she would have expected it to be. After all, she was under no illusions. She and Tom were colleagues now, nothing more than that. She didn't feature in his plans for the future and he didn't feature in hers. But it was funny that it should hurt so much when she understood that.

Tom saw her to the door shortly afterwards, repeating his thanks for her help. Lucy walked swiftly to the lift and stepped inside without looking back. There was no point in looking back, no point at all.

'Dr Farrell is going to operate tomorrow morning. He told me yesterday.' Emma Foster smiled as she stroked her daughter's hand through the porthole in the incubator. 'After that, all I can do is pray for a miracle.'

Lucy frowned. It was her first day back on duty after her break and she was catching up on what had been happening in her absence. Three babies had gone home but they'd had two new admissions, one of whom was the little girl who had been flown in by helicopter after the car crash. Lucy had been on her way to check on her when she had stopped to speak to Emma. Now, she couldn't help worrying about what Emma had said.

'You do realise that this operation won't cure Abigail, don't you?' she asked gently. 'All it will do is close the lesion on her spine.'

'Oh, yes. Dr Farrell explained all that, but you never know, do you? It might just sort things out.' Emma gave her a hopeful smile and Lucy didn't have the heart to press the point. However, she made a note to speak to Tom about it when she saw him.

Her heart gave a small lurch at the thought of seeing him again before she swiftly quelled it. If they could work together as colleagues, then that was all she could hope for, she reminded herself sternly as she carried on to her next tiny patient. However, all it took was the sound of his voice as he came into the unit to set it racing madly again. It took her all her time to gather her composure enough to greet him politely as he came over to join her.

'Good morning, Dr Farrell. I was just checking on baby Morrison,' she explained in a carefully neutral tone.

'That's who I wanted to see, too.' Tom frowned as he studied the tiny child in the incubator. 'I've been extremely concerned about her. Apart from the respiratory distress syndrome, she's hypoglycaemic and jaundiced as well.'

'She's not had the best start in life, has she?' Lucy observed softly, looking at the little girl. Like all very premature babies, she had little subcutaneous fat which gave her an oddly wizened appearance. Her skin was so thin that it was possible to see the network of veins beneath it. Her head and hands appeared disproportionately large compared to the rest of her body, but Lucy knew this was normal in an infant born so preterm, and wasn't an indication that there was anything wrong. However, the baby was suffering from several other worrying complaints, as Tom had said.

Respiratory distress syndrome was common in premature babies and potentially serious. A deficiency of surfactant, the chemicals which opened the tiny air sacs in the baby's lungs and allowed them to expand and contract easily, meant that she had difficulty breathing so she was being artificially ventilated and having surfactant therapy as well.

The incubator was maintaining her body temperature as, having such a low birth weight, she was unable to regulate it herself, and she was being fed through a nasogastric tube as she couldn't suck properly. Because her immune system wasn't fully developed there was the danger of infection, so she was being given antibiotic drugs intravenously plus iron and vitamin supplements. All in all, it was going to take a lot of skilful nursing to pull her through, but the fact that she had survived this long against such odds meant that she had a chance.

'Well, she seems to be holding her own, so that's one encouraging sign,' Tom said, unconsciously voicing her view. He took the child's notes from the end of the incubator to check through the previous night's obs.

'Mmm, that all looks OK. We'll just have to continue the treatment and keep our fingers crossed, basically. Still, every day she survives means that she's getting that bit stronger, so we'll try to be positive.'

'How is her mother? Have you heard?' Lucy asked as he put the notes back.

'She didn't make it, I'm afraid,' he said sadly. He sighed as he looked at the baby. 'The police haven't been able to trace any other family so far. It appears that the mother wasn't married and nobody knows who the father is.'

'So what's going to happen to her?' Lucy asked, glancing at the child.

'Social services are involved so I expect they will arrange foster care if nobody comes forward to claim her. The police are going to run an appeal in the papers over the next few days, asking for any relatives to get in touch, but they aren't all that hopeful. Poor little mite.'

He sounded upset but it didn't surprise her. Tom had always been genuinely concerned about the children he dealt with. She smiled as he looked at her quizzically, obviously sensing something from her expression. 'You always did take each case to heart.'

'I don't think it's possible not to feel something in a situation like this. Once you give up caring, then you may as well give up the job because it's all part and parcel of it, isn't it?' he replied softly.

She nodded. 'Yes, you're right about that. None of us would do this type of work if we didn't care.'

'Exactly.' He gave her a warm smile. 'That's why you are such an excellent nurse, Lucy, because you put your heart and soul into the job as well as your expertise. That's what makes all the difference.'

She was deeply touched by the compliment and looked away in case he saw how much it meant to her. 'Thank you. Now, who else do you want to see...? Oh, before I forget, I wanted a word with you about Emma Foster.'

'Is there a problem?' Tom frowned as he looked over to where Emma was sitting beside Abigail's incubator.

'I think there might be, but maybe it would be better if I explained it to you outside,' she said, glancing over her shoulder. She didn't want Emma overhearing what they were saying in case it upset her, but something needed to be done about the situation soon.

'Fine.' Tom obviously understood the need for privacy because he didn't question her. He checked his watch and grimaced. 'Actually, I could murder a cup of coffee if there's one going. I didn't have time with the rush to get Adam ready this morning, so I'm parched.'

'Well, that's easily sorted out.' She swiftly led the way to the door, pausing *en route* to tell Megan where she would be if she was needed.

'Okey-dokey. Take your time. There's no need to rush back.' Megan gave her an old-fashioned look which Tom obviously wasn't slow to see.

She hurried out of the unit, feeling the heat of embarrassment warming her cheeks. Fond as she was of Megan, she could cheerfully throttle her at times!

'What was that all about?' he asked as he caught her up. She steadfastly avoided his eyes. 'Nothing.'

'Oh, come on! There has to be a reason why Megan gave you that very knowing look just now. What's going on, Lucy? Why do I have the distinct feeling that I'm missing something?'

'You're not,' she said quickly, then sighed as she saw the scepticism on his face. 'Oh, all right! Megan discovered that you and I knew one another in Derbyshire, if you really want to know. I think she's been putting two and two together and coming up with all sorts of weird and wonderful answers!'

Tom folded his arms as he studied her flushed face. 'I take it that you haven't told her about us, then?'

'No, of course not!' she denied quickly. 'You know what hospitals are like. If anyone knew that you and I were...that we...'

She tailed off, wishing that she had chosen her words with more care. Suddenly the word she hadn't been able to actually come out and say seemed to be flashing in front of her in neon letters...

'Lovers?' He gave a deeply sardonic laugh which made the skin all over her body prickle with heat. 'I know it's hard to believe, but that's what we were once upon a time, isn't it?' He shrugged when she remained silent. 'I don't suppose anyone would be shocked in this day and age to find out that we'd had a bit of a fling, but I expect you were right to keep it to yourself. There is enough gossip in a hospital without us adding fuel to the fire.'

Lucy's pretty mouth compressed. *A bit of a fling!* Was that how Tom viewed it? Foolish or not, but it annoyed her intensely that he could be so dismissive of the time they had spent together.

'Precisely!' she snapped, her brown eyes sparkling as she glared at him. 'So I would appreciate it if you didn't say too much, either!'

'That's fine by me.' He smiled, although there was an odd expression in his eyes as he studied her flushed face. 'I'm as keen as you obviously are to keep my private life private, although maybe not for the same reasons.'

She wasn't sure what he meant by that, but it seemed unpropitious to ask when the answer might not be to her liking! She briskly led the way to the kitchen and plugged in the kettle, deeming it safer to let the matter drop, although that didn't mean she wasn't still annoyed. It most certainly hadn't been just a fling for her!

Tom followed her into the room and sat on the edge of the table, watching silently as she spooned instant coffee into two brightly patterned mugs. She was conscious of his gaze but steadfastly ignored it as she added boiling water then went to get the milk. It was rather cramped in the small kitchen so that she had to squeeze past him to reach the fridge. Her thigh brushed across his knee as she edged through the gap between the table and the sink unit and she felt a flurry of awareness race through her at the contact.

'Sorry.' He swivelled sideways to give her more room as she came back with the carton of milk. She gave him a thin smile, trying not to notice how the action had drawn the fabric of his trousers taut across his muscular thighs. Although he had lost weight recently, he still had the kind of leanly muscular physique which she had always found very attractive, and it seemed that she wasn't immune to his appeal even now!

Her hand shook as she put the mug on the table beside him so that coffee slopped over the side. She murmured an apology as she hurriedly fetched a cloth to mop it up, praying that Tom wouldn't guess why she was so nervous all of a sudden. So what if she *did* still find him attractive? She doubted he would appreciate it after what he had just said!

'Here, I'll do that.' He stood up to take the cloth from her at the same moment as she bent to wipe up the coffee, and they collided.

'Oops, sorry!' he apologised, quickly grasping hold of her as she staggered backwards. Lucy felt her breath catch as she felt the heat from his body flowing through the thin cotton of her uniform top as he steadied her against him. She shivered convulsively and felt him go absolutely still before abruptly he let her go. Picking up the cup, he took a swallow of the coffee, and there was something almost too studied about the way he did it.

Had he felt it, too? she wondered dizzily. Had he felt that same rush of heat which had invaded her limbs just now? It was impossible to tell, but just the thought that Tom might not be as indifferent to her as she'd imagined was enough to make her heart beat that little bit faster.

'So, what was it you wanted to tell me about Emma Foster?'

He set his cup down with a small thud which gained her immediate attention and she struggled to get her thoughts back on track and away from the dangerous path they were taking.

'I...I had a word with Emma earlier and she told me that Abigail is to be operated on tomorrow.'

'I have to say that I'm still in two minds whether it's the right thing to do.' Tom's tone was level in contrast to the tremulous note hers had held. When she glanced at him, she could tell by the thoughtful look on his face that his mind was focused solely on the problem of Emma Foster.

She bit her lip as she felt a bubble of hysterical laughter

well up inside her. Maybe he had been thinking about that all along and she had imagined his reaction just now? After all, he had grabbed hold of her purely to stop her falling over, not as an excuse to get her into his arms!

'What persuaded you to go ahead?' she asked flatly, determined that she wasn't going to make an even bigger fool of herself. The thought that Tom might have guessed how disturbed she'd been just now gave her hot and cold chills.

'Emma herself.' He sighed as he ran his hand round the back of his neck. Lucy could see real concern on his face and knew that he was extremely worried about the decision to operate on baby Abigail.

'She is so desperate for the baby to be given every chance possible, you see. I don't think I would have agreed if it weren't for that. The extent of the spinal lesions point firmly to the fact that Abigail is going to be severely handicapped if she survives. Frankly, the quality of life she can expect is going to be very poor,' he explained sadly.

Lucy sighed, understanding the quandary he was in. Trying to balance the needs of the baby and her mother's expectations wasn't easy in a case like this. 'I'm afraid that Emma has got it into her head that this operation might cure Abigail. She told me that she's going to pray for a miracle.'

'Unfortunately, that isn't going to happen. At best we'll keep the child alive, but that's as much as we can aim to do. Damn! I had a feeling that Emma might be setting her hopes too high, although I tried to make her understand the situation.'

She heard the frustration in his voice and knew that he blamed himself for Emma's unrealistic expectations. She hurried to reassure him that he wasn't at fault. 'Denial is common in a case like this, Tom. You know that. A lot of parents refuse to accept there is anything wrong with their child even though they can see the evidence for themselves.'

'I know that. But it's worse in this case because, all

through her pregnancy, I think Emma has been denying the fact that Abigail was going to be born handicapped. I spoke to her obstetrician and he said that they had tried umpteen times to make her understand, but she wouldn't listen.'

His face was full of compassion. 'Evidently, Emma suffered three miscarriages before she got pregnant with Abigail, so I think that must have had a huge bearing on why she refused a termination.'

'Oh, the poor thing! To have gone through all that as well.' Lucy's heart went out to the young woman for all that she had suffered.

'Exactly. It does help you understand why she went ahead and had Abigail, doesn't it? But it doesn't help the present situation and that's what we have to deal with now.' He sighed heavily. 'If only she could talk this all through with her husband, then maybe she would accept that Abigail is never going to be a normal child, but he hasn't even been to see the baby. I could happily wring his neck, if I got the chance, for leaving Emma to cope on her own like this!'

'Maybe we could try getting in touch with him and ask him to come in for a chat?' she suggested. She shrugged when she saw the sceptical look on his face. 'It can't hurt and it might just work. Emma needs to face up to the truth, and preferably before Abigail is operated on if the prognosis is so uncertain.'

'I suppose you're right. And, as you say, it can't hurt to try. Can I leave you to contact him, Lucy?' He gave a soft laugh and his expression was rueful. 'I'm sure you would be better at dealing with him than I would!'

She smiled at that. 'You know very well that you would handle it tactfully, Tom. That's one of your strengths, that, no matter how you feel inwardly, you don't show it.'

'I'm not sure I would agree it's a strength. Sometimes you lose out on an awful lot by not making your feelings plain.'

She wasn't sure what he meant by that, but before she

could question him Megan appeared. 'Sorry to interrupt but there's a call for you from Maddie Brooks in A and E, Dr Farrell. They've had a baby brought in, two weeks old and having seizures, and she wants to know if you can go down there a.s.a.p.?'

'Will do. Tell her I'm on my way, will you, Megan? Thanks.' Tom gulped down the rest of his coffee then headed for the door, pausing to glance back. 'I'll be back later to have a word with Emma to see if I can make her understand the situation better. OK?'

'Fine. Thanks, Tom... I mean, Dr Farrell,' Lucy amended quickly.

He shrugged. 'Tom will do fine. We don't want people thinking we've got something to hide by going too far the other way.'

'The other way...?' she began hesitantly.

'By being too circumspect.' He laughed deeply. 'You know how it is when people try too hard to deny there is anything going on—the old "we're just good friends" routine? We'd better not fall into that trap, Lucy. It would really get the gossip-mongers going!'

He hurried from the room and Lucy smiled as she went to the sink to wash their cups. He was probably right about that because, the more they tried to deny anything had happened in the past, the more people would start to wonder about it!

She sobered abruptly as a sudden thought struck her. What was there to wonder about, though? According to Tom it had been just a fling. It certainly hadn't been the most important period in his life as it had been in hers. Maybe in this case 'just good friends' meant precisely that!

CHAPTER FIVE

IT WAS a busy morning. The baby who had been brought in to A and E suffering a seizure was admitted and then they had a second child transferred to the unit from a hospital on the outskirts of the city. He had been born the previous night with Down's syndrome, which wasn't in itself a life-threatening condition. However, as he was also suffering from a congenital heart defect and intestinal atresia, the narrowing of a section of the intestines, it had been deemed wiser to send him to a specialist unit where he could receive maximum care.

He was to be operated on that very day. His father had accompanied him in the ambulance and Lucy took him into the office and gave him a cup of coffee while Lauren got the baby settled in.

'Thanks. It's all been such a shock, you understand. Mary and I had no idea that Jonathan was going to be...well, like he is.'

Lucy could understand that and sympathised. According to the case notes which had been faxed through, David and Mary Blake were both in their early twenties so they wouldn't have been offered screening for something like Down's, which tended to occur mainly when the mother was older. The fact that they already had one healthy child meant this had been an even bigger shock for them.

'It must have been. How has your wife taken it?' she asked gently.

'I'm not sure. It all happened so fast, you see.' He took a deep breath as he struggled to compose himself. 'I...I could tell as soon as he was born that there was something wrong even though nobody said anything to begin with. It was just the way the midwives looked at each other...'

He tailed off, obviously finding it painful to recall the moment. Lucy wished there were something she could say to make it easier for him, but there was nothing anyone could say in a situation like this. She just gave him time to collect himself, knowing that being able to talk would help.

'Anyway, they rushed Jonathan away and it seemed to be hours before the doctor came back and told us that he had Down's. We'd barely taken that in when he explained that he also had a heart defect and something wrong with his intestines, and that if he wasn't operated on immediately that he would die. I didn't know what to do, whether I should stay with Mary or come with him...'

He broke off once more and she hurried to reassure him. 'It's never easy in a situation like this, but I'm sure you've done the best thing possible under very difficult circumstances. Now, would you like to sit with Jonathan for a while? He will be going to theatre soon.'

'Yes, I would. Thank you.' He got to his feet and followed her back to the unit almost in a daze. Lucy fetched a chair and placed it beside the baby's crib.

'Now, if you need anything at all, Mr Blake, then just ring that bell and one of us will come straight away.' She showed him the bell on the wall next to the monitoring equipment.

'Thank you.' He looked round the room at the array of machinery the babies were attached to and shook his head. 'You never expect to see any of this, do you? You always assume that your baby is going to be fine.' He looked at his son and his face contorted with grief. 'Poor little devil. It doesn't seem fair, does it?'

There wasn't anything she could say so she gave him an encouraging smile, then left him with his son. This was one of the hardest parts of the job, she always thought, dealing with the parents' grief when things went wrong. However, she was confident that David Blake was the sort of man who would learn to cope once he had got over the shock, and be there for his wife when she needed him at this difficult time. If only all the fathers were like that!

Her gaze went to Abigail Foster and she couldn't help sighing. She had tried phoning Emma's husband several times throughout the morning but only succeeded in getting the answering machine each time. She had left a message for him to contact the hospital in the end, but whether he would respond to it was open to question. He certainly hadn't shown much interest so far!

She went for her lunch shortly afterwards, opting for the dish of the day, which was a delicious chicken and vegetable casserole which she had with salad. It wouldn't hurt to lose a few pounds, she decided, nobly turning her back on the chips.

Picking up her tray, she looked round the bustling canteen for somewhere to sit, smiling as Rob Turner waved and pointed to a free chair at his table. She went over to join him, wriggling her way between the tables, and plonked her tray down with a sigh of relief.

'I didn't think I was going to make that. Good job I've just decided to lose a few pounds. You need snake hips to get through this crush each day!'

Rob grinned as he forked up a mouthful of lasagne. 'Well, I suppose an inch here and there wouldn't go amiss...' He ducked as she aimed a playful cuff at his ear. 'Only kidding! You are absolutely perfect as you are, the Venus de Milo of women, Aphrodite reincarnated...'

'All right, all right! I'll let you off the hook, although I'm not sure I should be flattered by such comparisons,' she retorted as she sat down. 'From what I recall Aphrodite was rather amply endowed!'

'That's because the men in those days knew a good thing when they saw it,' Rob replied, not to be deterred. 'They liked their women to look like women! None of this dieting to within an inch of your life.'

He leered suggestively at her, making her laugh. 'Mmm,

sounds to me as though someone has kissed the Blarney
Stone this morning. Anyway, what would Meredith think
if she heard you saying that?' she teased. 'She might not
appreciate you handing out such lavish compliments!'

Rob shrugged as he stared at his plate. 'I don't imagine
she would care one way or the other.'

Lucy's brows rose. 'Sounds as though the course of true
love isn't running too smoothly. Problems?'

Rob sighed as he toyed with his lasagne. She had never
seen him looking so serious before so she knew that something was really troubling him. 'You could say that.
Meredith told me that she doesn't see any point in us going
out together any more.'

'I see. And was there a reason for that?' she asked quietly, wondering what could have gone wrong. Rob and
Meredith had seemed so happy together that she couldn't
imagine what had made the other woman take such a decision.

'She wouldn't tell me. I tried to get her to explain what
was wrong but she just clammed up.' Rob tossed his fork
onto his plate in a fit of impatience although she could see
the hurt in his eyes. 'Now she refuses to speak to me about
anything other than work. I can't make head nor tail of it,
to tell the truth. I thought that we were getting along fine
but it just goes to show how wrong you can be, doesn't
it?'

'I'm really sorry, Rob.' She reached over and squeezed
his hand. 'I thought that you and Meredith made a lovely
couple.'

'Me, too. Obviously we were both mistaken, weren't we?
Still, let's look on the bright side.' He raised her hand to
his lips and leered suggestively at her. 'I still have you, my
sweet. And, surely, you can find it in your heart to take
pity on me?'

She laughed as he'd intended her to although she wasn't
deaf to the pain in his voice. Meredith's rejection had hurt
him, no matter how he might be trying to make light of it.

'Mmm, that depends on what you mean by taking pity on you, Dr Turner!'

'Oh, dinner, dancing, followed by a wild night of passion—' he began in his most seductive tone, then broke off abruptly.

Lucy was chuckling so hard that she didn't realise why he had stopped. 'Followed by breakfast in bed, I suppose? Mmm, I get the picture, Rob. And I think you already know what my answer is going to be…'

She suddenly realised that he wasn't looking at her. She glanced over her shoulder and felt her heart ricochet around inside her chest as she saw Tom behind her. He gave her a thin smile before his gaze moved pointedly to where her hand was still tightly clasped in Rob's.

She immediately withdrew it, guilty colour washing up her face although she had no idea what she had to feel guilty about. She and Rob hadn't been doing anything wrong! Yet she couldn't help feeling uncomfortable when Tom looked at her that way.

'I'm sorry to interrupt your lunch, Dr Turner.' Tom had turned his attention to Rob now and his tone was icily polite. Lucy could tell that Rob was as disconcerted by it as she was. It was so unlike Tom to speak to anyone that way that she couldn't help wondering what was wrong.

'However, I thought you might like to sit in on the operation on the Down's baby this afternoon. It will be good experience for you, I imagine.'

'I…er… Yes. Thank you, sir.' Rob seemed to be having some difficulty getting his words out. However, before he could collect himself Tom bade them both a curt goodbye and went on his way.

Lucy watched him walking towards the door, his back rigid, his face set into such grim lines that she frowned in bewilderment. What on earth was the matter with him?

'Phew, talk about if looks could kill!'

Rob claimed her attention and she turned to him questioningly. He gave her a rueful grin. 'I didn't think the old grapevine had got it right this time, Lucy, but my mistake, eh?'

She frowned because she had no idea what he meant. 'Sorry, I'm not with you?'

'You and Tom Farrell. Rumour has it that you two were an item back in Derbyshire.' He shrugged when he saw her surprise. 'It doesn't take long for word to get round, as you very well know. I thought it was all so much hot air but obviously not. As I said, if looks could kill then I'd be on my way to the morgue right now!'

'Don't be silly, Rob. There's nothing between Tom and me, I can assure you. We were just…just good friends in Derbyshire, that's all,' she assured him, hoping that would convince him, but it had just the opposite effect.

Rob laughed out loud. 'Not that old story? Please!' He sobered abruptly as he glanced towards the door, although there was no sign of Tom now. 'Oh, hell, do you think he heard what I said about a night of passion? The last thing I need right now is to get on the wrong side of my new boss!'

He sounded really concerned so she hurried to reassure him. 'I'm sure he didn't. Anyway, you were only joking, not that it has anything to do with Tom even if you weren't. There is nothing going on between us, I promise you!' she repeated, but she could tell that Rob wasn't convinced.

The incident seemed to put rather a dampener on the conversation so that she wasn't sorry when Rob got up to leave shortly afterwards, using the excuse that he wanted to pop into the library to read up on the operation he was going to see that afternoon. It was obvious that he was uncomfortable with the idea that he might have got off on the wrong foot with Tom and that her reassurances had fallen on deaf ears.

Lucy sighed as she finished her lunch. It was ridiculous to imagine that Tom had been annoyed by what he had seen. So what if he had behaved rather oddly? Was that any reason to think that he had been jealous, as Rob seemed to believe?

She tried to brush off the thought but it lingered tantalisingly at the back of her mind. The most worrying thing of all was the fact that she felt rather pleased about it. It was good to imagine that Tom still cared...no matter how foolish it really was!

'I'd like a word with you about the Mitchell baby.'

Tom's tone was abrupt enough to make Lucy jump. She had been catching up on paperwork since she had got back from lunch and she hadn't heard him coming into the office. Now as she looked up and saw the chilly expression on his face she couldn't help having a few misgivings about what had happened earlier.

'The baby who was admitted this morning with a seizure?' she queried, trying to stop her mind whizzing off at tangents again. Tom couldn't care less what she did, she told herself sternly, but it wasn't as easy to convince herself as it should have been.

'Yes. I take it that you've had time to read through his notes?' He came into the room and closed the door but he didn't sit down. He had shed his suit jacket and he looked big and imposing as he stood in front of the desk staring down at her.

Lucy laid her pen on the blotter, feeling a little ripple of awareness run down her spine. The pale grey shirt he was wearing made his eyes look even darker in contrast, while the slim-fitting trousers emphasised the narrowness of his hips and the muscular length of his legs. Maybe she shouldn't be so aware of him, but she couldn't seem to stop herself noticing every detail. It was an effort to focus her thoughts on work and keep them there.

'Yes, I've read them. Evidently, the mother is a drug addict?'

'That's right. The baby is suffering from withdrawal symptoms. I've put him on chloral hydrate and phenobarbitone to control the seizures, but he is going to need very careful monitoring over the next few days. He isn't out of the woods yet and there is a very real danger of circulatory collapse,' he stated in the same coolly professional tone, which was beginning to irritate her.

'I realised that. I've put Lauren down to special him,' she replied equally coldly. 'He's on thirty-minute obs for the rest of the day and I shall inform the night staff that there might be a problem. Is that all? Or was there something else bothering you?'

His eyes narrowed as he caught the faint challenge in the question but he didn't respond to it. 'Frankly, yes. I'm worried about his parents or, to be precise, the possible disruption they might cause. We had a problem with them in A & E this morning. The father didn't want the child admitting, and created such a fuss that we had to call Security. I thought you should be warned.'

'I see. Well, I shall certainly be on my guard if they come to visit him, and I'll warn the others as well.' Lucy frowned. 'Why was the baby discharged from hospital so soon in the first place? I thought it was standard procedure, where the mother is a known drug user, to keep the child in under observation for a couple of weeks to avoid anything like this happening?'

'I got onto the hospital to check that out straight away.' Tom sighed. 'It appears that the mother walked out after a couple of days, taking the child with her. The hospital did get onto social services because they were so concerned, but when they sent someone to follow it up they discovered that she had given a false address.'

'What a stupid thing to do!' she declared in dismay.

'I know. Drug-withdrawal symptoms usually appear within the first forty-eight hours after birth. But in a few cases, like this one, it can be up to two weeks before there is any indication that something is wrong.' Tom's tone was grim. 'From what little I managed to get out of the mother this morning, the baby has been vomiting for the past couple of days and had bouts of diarrhoea as well.'

'If only she'd sought help sooner, then this might never have happened!' Lucy exclaimed sadly.

'Exactly. Anyway, I've been in touch with the hospital social worker. She is going to take advice on whether there is a strong enough case to have a protection order placed on the child,' he explained grimly.

'I take it that the parents don't know that yet?' She grimaced as he shook his head. 'Mmm, could be a tricky situation, then.'

'Which is why I want everyone to be extremely careful how they handle this. Obviously, we can't stop the parents seeing the baby until we are told otherwise, but they are to be supervised at all times.'

'You think they might try to remove him from here?' She couldn't hide her shock. 'Surely not! They must know how ill he is?'

'We're dealing with drug addiction here, Lucy. It isn't easy to tell how they will react in a case like this so we need to be on our guard. The baby's welfare is our first priority,' he stated flatly but she could tell how concerned he was about the situation.

'Of course. I understand. Poor little mite. It doesn't seem right, does it?'

'It doesn't. There are hundreds of people desperate for a child and yet here's a couple who have wilfully put their baby at risk when there was no need.' He was silent for a moment, then suddenly sighed. 'Anyway, just warn everyone to be extra careful, will you? By the way, did you manage to get in touch with Emma Foster's husband?'

She shook her head. 'There's no one answering the phone so I ended up leaving a message. I suppose he could be at work. I'll see if I can get the number from Emma, although I really didn't want to get her hopes up in case he refuses to come in.'

'Mmm, I can understand that. Has she any other family,

do you know? Maybe we could get in touch with a relative,' he suggested. 'I really think she needs someone with her at the moment.'

'I already thought of that. Apparently, both her parents are dead and there are no brothers or sisters either. It's the husband or nobody, I'm afraid.'

'Then all we can do is keep on trying to contact him.' Tom turned to leave. 'If you get a chance will you give it another shot this afternoon? Maybe you'll catch him then.'

'I'll try.' She hesitated, wondering if she should mention what had gone on that lunch-time. Tom hadn't made any reference to it but she felt that she should explain.

'Before you go, Tom, I just wanted to make sure that you hadn't got the wrong idea before,' she said quickly before her courage deserted her.

'I'm sorry?' He glanced back and his expression was so aloof once more that she was tempted to forget all about explaining what he had overheard. However, it stuck in her throat to imagine what he might be thinking!

'About me and Rob,' she said, then realised that might not have been the best way to begin so hurried on, 'I'm not sure how much of the conversation you overheard, but—'

'I'm sure that whatever you and Dr Turner get up to in your own time is your business.' His face was glacial as he opened the door. It was obvious that he had no intention of listening to what she was trying to say. 'I shall be in theatre for the rest of the day. Page me only if you think it's absolutely necessary.'

He had gone before she could draw breath to say anything else, not that she could think of much—or at least nothing at all professional! She swivelled her chair round and glared at the wall as she gave vent to her feelings. 'Of all the rude, pompous, arrogant, overbearing—'

'Oh, dear, someone's feathers seem to have been ruffled!'

She swung round at the sound of Megan's voice, her face

colouring as she saw the amused look her friend gave her.
Megan didn't even try to hide her laughter as she looked
pointedly along the corridor. 'Was that Dr Farrell I saw
leaving just now? It couldn't be him who's upset you, by
any chance?'

'I...er... No, of course not!' She quickly changed the
subject as she saw Megan's smile widen. 'Did you want
me for something?'

'The Blake baby is going to theatre now. Do you want
to have a word with Mr Blake beforehand?' Megan replied
in such a deliberately bland tone that Lucy's face flamed
even more.

'Yes, I think I should. The poor man is still rather dazed
by everything that's happened in the past few hours,' she
said briskly, getting up to walk to the door. Megan moved
aside to let her pass; she didn't say anything more on the
subject of Tom Farrell and whether he had been the cause
of her outburst. However, Lucy was conscious of the
amused looks Megan kept giving her for the rest of the
afternoon. In the circumstances, she could have done without them, but she realised that it would be playing into her
friend's hands if she tried to explain.

She experienced a momentary qualm as she thought back
to what Rob had said that lunch-time about the gossip
which was going round. It wasn't only Megan who was
putting two and two together, it seemed, and she wondered
what Tom would say if it reached his ears.

She sighed, realising what a mess it was turning out to
be. Most of the staff thought that she and Tom were an
item while Tom himself believed that she and Rob had
something going! When had life started to get so...so *complicated*?

'Oh, am I glad to get that over with! What a day.'

Sandra Parker spoke for all of them as they headed for
the staff room at the end of their shift. The busy morning
had been just a foretaste of what was to come. Sometimes

it just happened that all the babies became particularly fretful so that they'd had their work cut out attending to them. Then, to cap it all, Jack Williams had stopped breathing on no less than three occasions and needed resuscitating.

Rob had been paged but, before he had managed to get there from theatre, Meredith had appeared in response to the call. The atmosphere had dropped by a good ten degrees as the two had met up and it had taken a lot of tact on Lucy's part to smooth things over.

It had been a relief when Jack was stable once more and Rob and Meredith had gone their separate ways. Something obviously needed to be done about the situation, Lucy had decided, watching them leaving. But not that day. Frankly, they'd had enough to cope with without worrying about their star-crossed lovers!

She was as glad as everyone else that the day was finally over and was hurrying along the corridor when Kelly Morris, her opposite number on the night shift, called her.

'Lucy, do you know where Dr Farrell is, by any chance?'

She paused to look back. 'Probably still in theatre, I expect. Why? Is there a problem? He told me not to call him unless it was absolutely necessary,' she warned the other woman.

Kelly grimaced. 'Then I'm not sure what I should do. One of the staff from the crèche has just been on the phone to say that his little boy has bumped his head. It isn't serious but he's crying for his daddy and they wondered how long it was going to be before Dr Farrell went to collect him. I don't know if I should page him or not for something like this.'

'Oh, I think you should,' Lucy said quickly. 'Tom…I mean Dr Farrell would be most concerned if he wasn't told.'

'Well, I'll take *your* word for that, Lucy. I'll get a message to him right away, then.'

Kelly laughed as she went back inside the unit. It was obvious what she had meant and Lucy bit back a sigh as she realised that Rob had been right about the rumours. Still, there was little she could do to stop them so she would just have to wait until people got tired of talking about her and Tom. With no fuel to add to the fire, the flames would soon die down!

She changed into her outdoor clothes, then took the lift. The others had already left while she'd been speaking to Kelly so she was on her own. She was almost at the ground floor when it occurred to her that if Tom was still in theatre it might be some time before he could get away to see Adam. The thought of the little boy's distress was more than she could bear. Maybe she should pop into the crèche just to make sure that he was all right?

Ruth Jenkins, the crèche supervisor, looked surprised to see her when she rang the bell. 'What are you doing here?' she asked before her face cleared. 'Oh, you've come to check up on little Adam, have you? Great! Just what he needs at the moment, a familiar face.'

Ruth didn't give her chance to reply as she led the way inside. Lucy sighed ruefully. It seemed the rumours had spread even to this part of the hospital! She had a sudden misgiving about what she was doing, but all it took was the sight of Adam's tear-stained face to put that straight out of her head. It was obvious that the child was extremely upset about whatever mishap had befallen him, but his face lit up as soon as he saw her.

'Lucy!' He flung himself into her arms, clinging tight hold of her neck as she lifted him up.

'My, what a reception!' Ruth declared. She was in her late forties and had run the crèche for a number of years. All the parents spoke very highly of her because she was so good with the children and it was obvious that she was concerned about what had happened.

'It was only a bump, really. Adam and another little boy collided as they both ran to pick up one of the toys and banged their heads.' She showed Lucy the bruise on Adam's forehead, then lowered her voice.

'I'm certain there is nothing to worry about, but he got very upset when the mums and dads started arriving to take the other children home. He seemed to think that nobody was going to come for him, which is why I phoned up to find out where Dr Farrell was. Still, now that you're here, Lucy, everything's all right, isn't it, sweetie?' she added more loudly for Adam's benefit.

He nodded, although he didn't loosen his hold on Lucy's neck. She brushed a kiss over his cheek, her heart aching as she felt the dampness of tears on his skin. Adam's fear of being left possibly stemmed from the other night, when he had woken up to find himself alone in the flat, but she couldn't help wondering if there was another reason for it. However, it was impossible to ask the child that sort of question so she put it to the back of her mind.

'I'll stay until your daddy gets here, poppet,' she assured him.

He stared at her with solemn grey eyes which were uncannily like Tom's. 'Pwomise?'

'Promise!' she declared, smiling to hide the pain she felt. Adam was a miniature version of Tom and it made her heart ache to imagine how wonderful it would have been to watch him growing up. It brought it home to her once more how much she was going to miss by not having children of her own.

'Why don't you take Adam over there and sit down while you wait for Dr Farrell? That's the quiet corner where we read. Maybe he'd like you to read him a story?' Ruth suggested, pointing to a corner of the room where a few comfortable chairs were arranged around a coffee-table. There were several bookcases nearby, their shelves overflowing with brightly coloured picture books.

Lucy smiled. 'That sounds like a good idea to me. Do you want to show me which is your favourite book, Adam?'

'Uh-huh.' He hung on tightly as she carried him across the room, but once they were there he wriggled to be put down. He went straight to a bookcase and pulled a picture book off the shelf and took it back to her.

Lucy laughed when she saw what it was. '*Topsy and Tim's Tuesday Book*? That used to be my niece's favourite story, too! Come along, then, you sit on my knee and we'll read it together.'

He needed no further prompting as he climbed onto her knee. Lucy settled back in the chair to read him the story. It was obvious that he must have heard it many times before because he knew what was going to happen before she turned each page! They were reading it for the third time in succession when she suddenly became aware that some-one was watching them.

She looked up and felt her heart begin to thunder as she saw Tom standing a little way off. There was the strangest expression in his eyes at that moment which made her blood race, although she couldn't really understand what it meant. She was still trying to work it out when Adam sud-denly caught sight of him and scrambled down from her lap.

'I hurted my head and Lucy came and she's reading me a story. Look!' He thrust the book towards Tom, his small face alight with excitement as he regaled his father with everything that had happened.

Tom laughed as he ran a gentle hand over his son's head. 'You have had a busy day! You'll have to tell me all about it, but let me take a look at that bump on your head first.'

He crouched down and swiftly examined the small bruise on the child's forehead. Lucy was conscious that he hadn't spoken a word to her and her heart sank as it struck her that he might think she had been interfering by coming to see Adam without consulting him first.

'I thought it might be a while before you managed to get out of theatre,' she hurriedly explained as he stood up. 'I just popped in to make sure he was all right. I hope you don't mind?'

'Of course I don't mind!' He must have seen the start

she gave because he sighed. 'Sorry. I didn't mean to snap. It's just that I've been going through agonies imagining how upset he was going to be when I didn't turn up. I really appreciate you coming to see him, Lucy. Thank you.'

He swung the little boy into his arms and smiled at him with such tenderness that it brought a lump to her throat. 'Say thank you to Lucy, tiger.'

'Thank you,' the child repeated obediently, then suddenly reached over and grabbed hold of her round the neck while he planted a noisy kiss on her cheek.

'Wow, what a smacker!' she declared, deeply touched by the show of affection. She smiled at Tom and suddenly realised how close they were now that Adam had an arm around both their necks...

She took a quick breath as her heart began to race. There was something in his eyes at that moment which made the blood rush through her veins even though she wasn't sure what she was seeing. He had stated so categorically that he wanted to forget about their past and yet when he looked at her that way, with such tenderness, it seemed to make a mockery of all that—

'Daddy, kiss Lucy!' Adam's voice abruptly broke the spell and she started as she realised what he had said. A wash of colour ran up her face as she quickly tried to disentangle herself, but he held on tightly as he repeated his request.

'Kiss Lucy, Daddy!'

'How can I refuse?' Tom's face was full of amusement as he bent and kissed her on the cheek. It was no more than a token yet she felt the ripple of awareness which ran through her as she felt the cool brush of his lips against her skin. She turned away as Adam released her, making a great production out of picking up her bag so that Tom couldn't see how much the kiss had disturbed her. She had been kissed many times, but nobody had ever been able to make her feel the way Tom could make her feel!

It was an effort to act naturally when she heard Adam

utter an excited exclamation but there was no way that she wanted Tom to suspect there was anything wrong.

'Somebody sounds happy,' she observed lightly.

'I've just told him that I'll take him for a burger as a treat,' he explained. He grinned conspiratorially. 'It also means that I won't have to set to and make tea when we get in!'

'Ah-h-h, I see. Method in the madness, is there?' she teased, genuinely amused by the wry confession.

'Something like that—' He broke off as Adam started tugging on his sleeve.

'Can Lucy come?' the little boy demanded eagerly.

'Oh, no, really—' she began, not wanting Tom to feel that he had to invite her. However, he cut in smoothly before she had time to finish.

'Lucy might be too busy to come, Adam,' he said flatly, yet there was a nuance in his voice which made her frown when she heard it. Oh, she could appreciate that he might not want her to join them, and was offering her a way to turn down the invitation without upsetting the child, yet there had seemed to be something more behind that statement...

She gasped as she realised what it was. Tom obviously believed that she had made plans to see Rob Turner that night. What was it that Rob had suggested at lunch-time—dinner, dancing? Not to mention a night of passion, of course!

Her spine stiffened as she stared him straight in the eyes. It annoyed her intensely that he should have taken the light-hearted conversation so literally and then refused to listen to her attempts to explain! 'Actually, I don't have any plans for this evening, Tom. I wonder what made you think that I had?'

His eyes darkened as she threw the challenge at him yet it wasn't annoyance which shimmered in their depths, as she might have expected. She felt her pulse leap as she realised that it was relief which had altered their colour so dramatically. She was just trying to get to grips with that idea so that it was little wonder that she didn't have her wits fully about her as he answered.

'In that case, there is no reason why you can't come with us, is there?' He didn't give her time to reply before he turned to Adam. 'OK, burgers and fries for three coming right up!'

'Yes!' Adam raced towards the door, obviously thrilled by the news. Lucy took a quick breath as she realised there was no way she could refuse to go now without upsetting him. She followed Tom to the door, trying to ignore the looks being cast their way by those members of staff who had arrived to collect their offspring, but it was obvious what they were thinking.

She bit back a sigh. Nothing could be more innocent than a trip to a burger bar, but she'd bet a month's salary that the story would take on a whole new dimension once the gossips got to work!

CHAPTER SIX

'My ears are throbbing! What a din!'

Tom's tone was so rueful that Lucy couldn't help laughing. 'It's hard to believe that a few children can make this much noise, isn't it?'

'It is indeed! And here I was thinking about giving Adam a party for his birthday, too.' He shuddered expressively but she could see the amusement on his face. 'I must be mad! Can you imagine what a dozen four year olds could get up to racing around the flat?'

'I don't need to imagine it,' she replied tartly. 'I've helped my sister enough times when she's given Jessica a party to *know* the sort of chaos they can cause!'

She smiled as she looked round the restaurant. Most of the noise was coming from a group of children in the far corner of the room who were obviously celebrating the birthday of one of them. The restaurant had hired a clown to entertain them and they were all very excited. Little Adam had wandered over to watch and was staring wide-eyed as the clown plucked chocolate coins from behind several of the children's ears.

Lucy's face softened as she saw how fascinated he was by what was happening. 'You could always do what those parents are doing and hold Adam's party here?' she suggested, glancing at Tom. 'When is his birthday, by the way?'

'Next month, the nineteenth,' he replied, looking across the room and mercifully missing the shadow which crossed her face. 'That's a good idea, actually. I had planned on holding it at home and invite some of the youngsters he knows from the crèche, but it would be a lot less work if I held it here, wouldn't it?'

'It certainly would,' she agreed flatly. She took a quick breath but it hurt to be reminded that he must have married Fiona so soon after they had split up. It just went to prove that he could never really have loved her, otherwise he wouldn't have married the other woman so quickly.

She quickly pushed that thought to the back of her mind as Adam came back to the table and picked up his cup of cola. 'Careful,' she warned, helping him hold it steady as he drank. He gave her a wide smile before he ran back to watch the clown. He seemed to have got over his earlier upset and, apart from the occasional glance round to make sure they were still there, seemed quite happy to watch what was going on.

Lucy frowned as she recalled how scared he had been when she'd arrived at the crèche. Maybe it wasn't her place to mention it but she couldn't help wondering why the little boy was so insecure. 'Why is Adam so afraid of being left? Was it what happened the other night?'

Tom sighed as he turned to her. 'I think that simply added to his fears.' He glanced at his son and she was shocked to see the anger which crossed his face. 'It wasn't the first time that he had been left by himself, you see. The day Fiona died she had left him in the house on his own. It was some time before the police managed to contact me. I went straight home as soon as I discovered Adam wasn't with her, but he was very upset, as you can imagine.'

'He must have been. Poor little thing!' Lucy exclaimed, trying to hide her dismay. She couldn't begin to imagine why Adam's mother had left him on his own, because it was something she certainly wouldn't have done.

'Had Fiona just popped out on an errand when the accident happened?' she asked curiously, wondering if that was the explanation.

'Apparently.' Tom's tone was flat as he confirmed her suspicion, so she couldn't explain why she had a feeling there was something he wasn't telling her. When Adam came running back to the table, he immediately changed the subject.

She sighed as he picked up Adam's jacket and started to get him ready to leave. Frankly, it wasn't any of her business and Tom wouldn't appreciate her asking him any more questions. But that didn't stop her being curious, of course.

They left the restaurant and walked back towards the park. The worst of the rush hour was over and, once they were away from the main streets, it was a little quieter. Adam walked along between them, holding their hands. However, it soon became obvious that he was getting tired because his feet started to drag.

Tom swung the child up into his arms, smiling as Adam gave a huge yawn. 'I think a bath and bed are the only things left on the agenda for you tonight, young man. You're absolutely worn out.'

'Adam have story?' the little boy put in quickly. He turned to Lucy and smiled blithely. 'Lucy read it.'

Tom grimaced as he looked at her. 'You seem to have a fan here, I'm afraid. Would you mind? Say no if you're in a rush to get back.'

'Of course I don't mind,' she declared truthfully. 'But there is one condition—not *Topsy and Tim's Tuesday Book*!'

Tom laughed deeply. 'Mmm, he does tend to have a one-track mind! But we'll choose something else for tonight, eh, Adam?'

Adam nodded solemnly. '*Wednesday Book.*'

He looked surprised when they both laughed. She shot an amused glance at Tom. 'One-track mind, as you say!'

'That's my boy!' He grinned back at her, the dimple in his lean cheek dancing in and out. He looked so much like the old Tom she remembered that she felt her breath catch. It was an effort to act naturally as they carried on walking, but there was no way she could prevent her mind from spinning wild little fantasies. Five years didn't seem such an awfully long time after all…

'Asleep at last!'

Lucy breathed a sigh of relief as she crept from the bedroom. She paused to glance back, a smile lighting her face as she looked at the little boy curled up under the duvet. 'Considering how tired he was, he still managed to hang on till the very last page!'

'Adam is a very determined child. When he sets his mind to something he sticks to it.'

Tom laughed softly as he looked at his son with a mixture of pride and amusement. He pulled the bedroom door to then looked at her with a faint lift of his dark brows. 'How about a glass of wine after all that hard work? Your throat must be dry as a bone after reading to him for so long.'

'Well…' She hesitated a moment but there seemed no reason to refuse. 'That would be lovely. Thanks.'

'Great. You go and sit yourself down while I open a bottle. Red or white, by the way?' he added as an afterthought.

She shrugged. 'I don't mind. I'll leave it up to you.'

'Fine.' He gave her a quick smile then headed towards the kitchen. Lucy went into the lounge and sat down on the sofa, kicking off her shoes as she made herself comfortable. Tom came back a few minutes later with a bottle and two glasses which he set on the coffee-table.

'I decided on white because you always preferred it,' he said as he began to fill the glasses.

She smiled. 'I'm surprised you remembered after all this time,' she said without thinking.

His hand stilled although he didn't look at her. 'There's a lot of things I remember, Lucy.'

She wasn't sure what to say to that so stayed silent, afraid that she might be reading too much into the remark. It had been said just in passing and hadn't really meant anything,

she assured herself. But it was surprisingly difficult to believe that. It was a relief when he handed her a glass then
got up to put a CD on the stereo.

She frowned as she struggled to identify the piece. 'Is it
Vivaldi?'

'That's right. From "The Four Seasons". Do you remember when we went to that outdoor concert that time?
They played it then,' Tom replied, picking up his glass.
There was nothing in his voice to explain it but she felt a
little shiver run down her spine as he reminded her of the
occasion.

The concert had been held in the grounds of a stately
home close to the hospital in Derbyshire where they had
both been working at the time. Lucy had gone along with
a group of friends and they had joined forces with Tom's
party when they'd met up there.

It had been a glorious summer's evening and everyone
had enjoyed themselves immensely. They had taken picnics
to eat, not the usual run-of-the-mill sandwiches, but something more fitting to the occasion. She had splurged on
smoked salmon as her contribution and Tom had brought
along some champagne, which had been greatly appreciated.

It had been a truly magical night, made all the more
special because it had been then that Tom had first asked
her out on a date. Now, as she thought back to it, she felt
overwhelmed by sadness. That night had been the beginning of the most wonderful time in her life but a few
months later it had been over.

It was an effort to keep her tone light as she struggled
with the thought. 'It was a great night, wasn't it? It's hard
to believe that we were so lucky with the weather!'

He laughed deeply but there was an expression in his
eyes which told her that he too remembered what had happened that night. 'It is, especially when you think about the
rotten summer we had last year. Did you manage to get
away for a holiday?'

'I just had a week at my sister's.' She shrugged, glad that the conversation had moved away from such a fraught topic. 'I moved into a new flat last year so money was rather tight and I simply couldn't afford to go on holiday. The down side of living in London is that it costs a fortune to rent anywhere decent.'

'Don't I know it!' Tom agreed wryly, looking around him. 'I was horrified when I discovered how much this place was going to cost but I needed to be close to work because of Adam. I didn't want to spend hours each day commuting and end up getting home after he'd gone to bed.'

'It's a problem when children are so young, isn't it? Still, when he gets older you can probably look further afield?' she suggested.

'That's what I'm hoping. I'd like to get somewhere with a garden for him to play in,' he explained. 'Fortunately, we have the park virtually on our doorstep here, but it isn't the same. Where do you live? I only got your number off Imogen Drew the other day when I needed to phone you.'

He suddenly laughed. 'Actually, I was extremely lucky to get that! She was very reluctant to part with any information. It took Martyn Lennard's intervention to prise your phone number out of her. He had to vouch for me!'

Lucy laughed at that. The Principal Nursing Officer, Imogen Drew, was a stickler for the rules, and Lucy could imagine her reaction to Tom's request for her phone number. 'I live in Bayswater. I've a tiny basement flat there. And, yes, you're right that Mrs Drew is very careful where her nurses are concerned.' She gave him a deliberately innocent smile. 'She doesn't give out information to just any Tom, Dick or Harry!'

Tom winced at the pun. 'Oh, please! I'd forgotten about your rotten jokes, Lucy!'

'My rotten jokes?' She glared at him, thinking how attractive he was when he laughed like that. Laughter softened the rather austere lines of his face and gave a glimpse of the man she remembered, a man who once upon a time had seemed to have a knack for taking from life as much as he'd put into it. Tom had *enjoyed* life so much when they'd been together and she found herself smiling as she recalled those days.

'I think that's a real cheek coming from someone who once stood up in front of an audience and regaled them with jokes such as "What is yellow and dangerous?" she declared loftily.

'Shark-infested custard!' Tom was quite unabashed as he promptly delivered the punchline. 'Well, they always say the old ones are the best, don't they?'

'And you can't get much older—or cornier!—than that,' she shot back.

He grinned. 'You are just being picky now. Anyway, the audience seemed to enjoy my jokes that day, so what are you complaining about?'

'The audience enjoyed them because they had to! Once you'd got everyone in the hall that time, then you had no intention of letting us go until you'd raised the money you needed for that new equipment for the children's ward,' she declared, refusing to give an inch. 'What did you charge, now…fifty pence for each joke you told? We were a captive audience in more ways than one, so we had to make the best of it!'

Tom chuckled as he picked up the bottle to refill their glasses. 'It worked, though, didn't it? We raised close to five hundred pounds that day. And as for the quality of the jokes, well, I can't claim all the credit for that. Most of the children on the ward contributed to my script, plus their mums and dads added a few suggestions, although some of them had to be censored because of the tender age of certain members of the audience! It was a real team effort, I'd say.'

'It was indeed.' She smiled reminiscently. 'Do you remember how excited the kids were when you told one of their jokes? A few who weren't too sick were allowed out of bed to watch the show and I can still remember their faces to this day.'

She looked at Tom and was surprised by the look of sadness on his face at that moment. 'Yes, I remember. It was a great day, wasn't it? But we had a lot of good times back then, as I recall.'

She shivered as she heard the wistful note in his voice as he unconsciously reiterated what she had been thinking a few minutes earlier. They had had a lot of fun and it was hard not to think about how much she had missed that aspect of their relationship in the past few years.

'More wine?' Tom held up the bottle but she shook her head, knowing that it would be foolish to prolong the evening. It was too painful to keep thinking about the past all the time, but it was hard not to when they were together like this.

'No, thanks. That was lovely, but I think I'd better be on my way.'

She drained her glass then stood up to leave, fixing a bright smile into place so that he wouldn't guess how she was feeling. 'If only' were the two saddest words in the whole language, but it was hard not to use them in this context.

'Thanks for inviting me tonight, Tom. I really enjoyed it,' she said quickly, praying that he wouldn't hear the catch in her voice.

'Thank you for coming.' He took a deep breath and even as she watched the warmth faded from his eyes. 'I know that Adam enjoyed having you with us.'

'Good. That's the main thing,' she replied brightly. Did Tom *really* need to make it plain that he had only invited her for Adam's benefit? she wondered, turning away before he saw how much it had hurt her, but she wasn't quick enough.

'Is something wrong, Lucy?' he asked, putting a detaining hand on her arm as she went to hurry out to the hall.

'Of course not!' she denied, but she could tell by the frowning look he gave her that he wasn't convinced.

'Are you sure?' He bent to look at her with real concern and suddenly the words came tumbling out before she could stop them.

'I realised that you only invited me tonight for Adam's sake,' she said tightly. 'So there is no need to worry that I'll get the wrong idea, Tom!'

He went completely still. Lucy guessed that he was struggling to find something to say and suddenly she couldn't bear to listen to any polite denials.

'Forget it!' she said hoarsely, trying to shrug his hand off, but he wouldn't let her go. He swung her round to face him and his eyes were very dark as they stared straight into hers.

'Yes, I did invite you for Adam's sake,' he stated with more than a hint of impatience. He took a quick breath and she saw myriad expressions cross his face as he continued in a grating tone which made her heart catch. 'But I'd be lying if I said that I hadn't enjoyed this evening, Lucy.'

'I…' She stopped as soon as she'd begun because suddenly she didn't know what to say. Anything seemed either too much or too little at that moment. She looked into Tom's eyes and saw there all the turmoil she felt. Was he as mixed up as she was? Did he wish that things could have turned out differently for them? Did Tom wish that they…they could turn back the clock and try again?

She could only stand there and stare at him with eyes which betrayed all the uncertainty she felt. She heard him utter something rough under his breath before he suddenly drew her towards him. She knew that he was going to kiss her and part of her mind was crying out that it would be a mistake to let it happen, only the other part refused to listen.

She closed her eyes, praying she would find the strength to be sensible if she didn't look at him, but it was the wrong thing to do. Without the benefit of sight to dilute them, her other senses became unnaturally acute so that things she would otherwise not have noticed seemed to assail her. The clean fresh scent of his skin made a shiver ripple down her spine as she inhaled it, whilst the warmth of his breath on her cheek made every cell in her body feel as though it were suddenly on fire.

She gave a small, shocked murmur as she tried to blank out the sensations, but just at that moment she heard the uneven rasp of his breathing, felt her own breathing alter to mimic his.

Her eyes flew open in panic but it was already too late to do anything as his mouth found hers and all thoughts of being sensible fragmented the very instant she felt the firm pressure of his lips. Suddenly, everything seemed to distil to this one moment when Tom kissed her, as though the past five years had never happened…

'Daddy!'

The frightened cry from the bedroom made them both jump. There was a moment when Tom still held her, as though he couldn't bear to let her go, and then his hands fell to his sides as she stepped back.

'That's Adam. I…I'd better go and see if he's all right.'

Lucy nodded because she didn't trust herself to speak. It took her all her time just to stand there as he swung round on his heel and strode towards the bedroom. He disappeared inside and she heard the murmur of voices—Adam's high, childish one, Tom's deeper one soothing him. Tears stung her eyes as she realised how foolish she had been.

The past five years couldn't be erased! What had happened during them most certainly couldn't be. Tom had married and had the child he had always longed for. He had found everything he had wanted with another woman. When he went to bed at night it would be Fiona he dreamt about, their time together he must wish he could have all over again! How could what *they* had shared ever measure up to that?

She took her coat off the peg and let herself out without waiting for him to come back. There was no point. She was only fooling herself by thinking that Tom might long for the days they had spent together. His life had only really begun after they had parted.

'Mmm, so what's this I hear about you and our dishy new boss?'

Lucy was going into work the following morning when Megan hurried up behind her. She looked round, trying to stifle a sigh as she saw the curiosity on the other woman's face. A restless night spent going over and over everything that had happened had taken its toll and she could have done without having to deal with whatever was on Megan's mind at that moment!

'I don't know what you mean,' she said shortly, whisking through the doors and praying that her friend would take the hint. However, it was obvious that Megan had no intention of letting the subject drop as they made their way to the lifts.

'Oh, come on, Lucy! I just met Jilly Howard and she said that she saw you and Tom Farrell in a burger bar last night looking very cosy. Do I detect a hint of romance in the air?'

'I've no idea what you can smell but I assure you it isn't romance!' she retorted, inwardly groaning. She couldn't recall seeing Jilly in the restaurant, but then the place had been extremely crowded.

The lift arrived at that moment so she stepped inside and pressed the button for their floor. 'Anyway, I'd say it's a contradiction in terms to say that Tom and I looked ''cosy'' in a burger bar!'

Megan laughed at that but Lucy could tell that she hadn't been deterred. 'Mmm, well, it isn't my idea of the perfect spot for a romantic dinner, but then I believe you had Dr Farrell's little boy with you. Dining *en famille* now, are you? Things are hotting up!'

Lucy shook her head. 'You are a really sad case, Megan Whittaker, if you can make something out of this. All right, so I did go and have a burger with Tom and Adam last night. That's it…period!'

'And that's why you've got those bags under your eyes this morning?' Megan smiled knowingly. 'Listen, you're talking to someone who's been into more burger bars than she cares to count and, take it from me, the only thing I ever end up with is indigestion! I certainly don't come into work the next morning looking as though I'd had a wild night out on the town!'

Lucy raised her eyes to the heavens. 'I give up! What can I say to convince you that it was as innocent as it sounds?'

'Mmm, I bet that was what Nikki Barclay kept saying, and look what happened to her!' Megan retorted with a grin.

Lucy groaned. 'You have an answer for everything! Just because Nikki fell head over heels in love with David Campbell while he was over here doesn't mean that you can start letting your imagination run away with you!'

'It was *so* romantic, though, wasn't it?' Megan sighed. 'I heard that the wedding was lovely.'

'So did I. St Alban's Cathedral is such a beautiful building and I believe that Nikki looked fabulous. David's niece, Jazzy, was chief bridesmaid and Nikki asked two of her patients from the rheumatology unit to be her flowergirls.' Lucy laughed. 'Evidently, Susan and Emma haven't stopped talking about it ever since!'

'I bet it was a great day for them. It's a shame we were working and couldn't go to watch. I'll miss Nikki now that she and David are off to Australia to live.' Megan squared her shoulders. 'But let's not get sidetracked. We were discussing you and Tom Farrell, not Nikki and David.'

Lucy rolled her eyes. 'There is nothing to discuss! How many more times do I have to tell you that? We went for a burger, then I went back and read Adam a story and that was it!'

She realised immediately that had been the wrong thing

to say. Admitting that she had gone back to Tom's flat had been a big mistake! Mercifully, they reached their floor just then so she hurried out of the lift before Megan could start to cross-examine her. Frankly, she could do without the third degree at that moment! It was a relief when Kelly Morris, who had been working the night shift, came rushing along the corridor as soon as she saw her.

'Oh, am I glad to see you!' she exclaimed.

Lucy frowned. 'Why? What's happened?'

'Abigail Foster died an hour ago. She started to deteriorate around midnight so we sent for the night reg but there was nothing he could do,' Kelly explained sadly.

'Oh, no, what a shame.' Lucy glanced at Megan, who grimaced. She turned back to Kelly. 'How has Emma taken it?'

'That's why I'm so glad to see you.' Kelly sighed heavily. 'We can't seem to make Emma understand that Abigail is dead. She's just sitting in her room rocking Abigail in her arms and singing to her.'

Kelly sounded really upset. She hadn't worked in neonatal intensive care very long and Lucy knew that she had little experience of this kind of situation. 'Can you have a word with her, Lucy? Sister has tried talking to her but even she couldn't seem to get through to her. And, as for me, I just don't know what to say, to be frank.'

'Of course, if you think it will help.' She gave the other woman a commiserating smile as she handed Megan her coat to take to the staff room. 'It's never easy to know what to say in a situation like this, Kelly, so don't feel bad about it.'

'I know we covered this on our course, what to do in the case of a baby dying, but this is different.' Kelly still looked worried as Lucy accompanied her along the corridor. 'All along I've had a feeling that Emma has been refusing to face the fact that the baby might die.'

'I know what you mean,' she agreed sadly. She paused outside Emma's room. 'Look, can you do me a favour and

have Dr Farrell paged as soon as he arrives? It might help
if he had a word with Emma.'

'Will do.' Kelly looked relieved to have relinquished the
problem to someone else as she hurried away. There was
a general air of bustle about the place as the night staff got
ready to hand over to their daytime colleagues. Lucy
guessed that they would be glad to get off home after what
had happened.

The death of a baby was upsetting for everyone concerned, but sometimes no amount of skilled care could prevent the inevitable. Now she just wanted to make it as easy
as possible for Emma, but she suspected that it was going
to take a lot of patience and support to help her come to
terms with her daughter's death.

She knocked on the door before she went into the room.
Emma was sitting by the window and she looked round as
she heard her. 'Shh,' she warned, putting a finger to her
lips. 'Abigail's just dropped off to sleep so mind you don't
wake her.'

Lucy went over to her, feeling her heart aching as she
looked at the baby. Abigail had been wrapped in a lacy
shawl and to all intents and purposes looked as though she
were merely asleep. It was normal practice to allow the
parents to hold their child after it had died. Many had told
her how invaluable it had been in helping them come to
terms with their loss. However, Emma's refusal to accept
that her baby was dead was something which needed careful handling.

'She's very beautiful, Emma,' she said softly, turning
back a fold of shawl so that she could look at the tiny doll-
like face. 'You'll be able to remember her this way, won't
you?'

Emma's arms tightened as an expression of panic crossed
her face. 'You're not going to take her away from me!'

'Of course not. You can hold Abigail for as long as you
want to,' she assured her. 'But you know that she isn't
really sleeping, don't you? Abigail was very sick, too sick

to get better. She might have been in a lot of pain if she'd lived, but now she won't have to go through any of that.'

Two huge tears slid down Emma's cheeks. 'I don't want her to be dead,' she muttered thickly. 'Make someone do something…that doctor…what's his name?'

'Dr Farrell,' Lucy said quietly. She laid her hand on Emma's arm and made her look at her. 'Dr Farrell can't do anything for Abigail, I'm afraid. Nobody can. I know it's hard, Emma, but you have to accept that.'

She looked round as the door opened and Tom appeared. Emma didn't seem to be aware of him as she bent over the baby and began crooning to her. Lucy shot her a worried look before she went to speak to him.

'I'm extremely worried about her,' she said without any preamble, although she couldn't help noticing how tired he looked. There were dark circles under his eyes and lines bracketing his mouth. Her concentration wavered as she found herself wondering if what had happened the previous night was responsible for them. Was Tom feeling guilty about kissing her? Did he regret it? The thought made her heart ache but it was neither the time nor the place to dwell on it right then.

'Emma refuses to accept that Abigail is dead,' she explained quietly, lowering her voice so that the other woman couldn't hear her.

Tom sighed heavily as he looked across the room. 'I was afraid this might happen. I've asked Sandra to get in touch with her GP; she is going to need an awful lot of support over the coming weeks.'

'We have our own support group here at the hospital for cases like this,' Lucy reminded him. 'I'll get onto them as well. But that doesn't solve the immediate problem of making Emma accept what has happened.'

'I'll have a word and see if I can get through to her.' Tom frowned. 'I don't suppose you had any luck with her husband?'

'He didn't reply to the message I left on the answering machine.'

'Can you give him another ring, then, Lucy?' Tom glanced at his watch. 'He might be there at this time of the morning. Regardless of what the situation is between him and Emma, he needs to be told about this, of course.'

'Will do.' She turned to leave, but Tom put his hand on her arm to stop her.

'Did you get home all right last night? I was going to ring for a taxi for you but you'd already gone when I finished settling Adam down.' His tone was flat so that she had no idea what he was thinking.

'I…I thought it best if I didn't stay, Tom,' she said quickly. 'Was Adam all right, by the way?'

'Fine. He'd had a bad dream but he settled down again without much trouble.' He looked away and she saw him take a deep breath before he continued. 'About last night, Lucy, I think I owe you an apology.'

'An apology?' she repeated blankly and saw his mouth thin.

'For what happened, of course. I never intended to…to compromise you in any way and I apologise for it.'

There was no mistaking the regret in his voice and her heart felt like a leaden weight as she realised that her suspicions had been correct. Tom *did* feel guilty about kissing her. He probably saw it as a betrayal of his wife and everything he had felt for her. It hurt so much to realise that and know how he was torturing himself.

'Don't worry about it,' she said with forced brightness. 'Put it down to too much wine and an overdose of nostalgia!'

His hand fell from her arm and he laughed deeply. 'I expect you're right. A lethal combination, aren't they? I don't suppose we're the first poor souls who've succumbed to them either. Still, no harm done?'

'None at all,' she replied softly, struggling to maintain her smile.

He gave her a brief nod then went over to speak to Emma. Lucy quickly left the room as tears misted her eyes. In her heart she had known that kiss hadn't really meant anything, but that didn't make it any less painful to hear Tom admit that!

CHAPTER SEVEN

IT WAS mid-morning when Emma's husband finally arrived. Lucy had managed to catch him at home and explained what had happened. He hadn't said much in response to the news that Abigail had died but he had agreed to come into the hospital. She was in the office when Lauren brought him to see her.

'Please come in, Mr Foster,' she invited, taking swift stock of him as he sat down. He was in his early-thirties and possessed the sort of boyish good looks which many women would find attractive, she suspected. He was dressed for the office in a smart pinstriped suit and she couldn't help wondering how any man could put his job first at a time like this. However, it wasn't her place to be judgemental so she confined herself to the reason he was there.

'We are all very sorry about your daughter, Mr Foster—' she began but he curtly interrupted her.

'It was the best thing that could have happened,' he stated bluntly. 'If I'd had any idea there was going to be something like this wrong with the baby then I'd have made certain that Emma got rid of it.'

Lucy had to bite her tongue, although it wasn't unknown for parents to take this view. Some were never able to accept their child's handicap and Emma had been wrong to keep it a secret from him. However, she was more concerned about the effect his attitude might have on Emma in her present state of mind.

'It's never easy when a baby is born so severely handicapped. However, it's Emma who concerns us at the moment. She's refusing to accept that the baby is dead even though we have done our utmost to make her understand what has happened,' she explained levelly. 'I'm sure that now you're here you will be able to help her come to terms with it.'

Peter Foster glanced impatiently at his watch as he stood up. 'I've a meeting at twelve so I can't stay long. I'll see what I can do but, frankly, I've neither the time nor the patience for this when it could have been avoided.

'I may as well be straight with you: our marriage was on the rocks even before this happened. I only stayed with her because she was expecting the baby. Now there isn't much point in keeping up the pretence, is there?'

Lucy's heart sank. She didn't dare imagine what would happen to Emma if her husband walked out on her at this point. It took her all her time to keep her thoughts to herself as she showed Peter Foster to Emma's room.

She closed the door, sending up a prayer that he would show a *bit* of sensitivity, but she wasn't all that hopeful. Maybe it had been a mistake, after all, to ask him to come in? She made a note to tell Tom about it as soon as possible but he didn't appear before she went for her lunch. Lauren went with her and it soon became obvious that she had heard the latest bit of gossip.

'So what's this I hear about you and Tom Farrell being spotted out together last night?' she demanded as soon as they sat down.

Lucy sighed. 'Megan should know better than to go spreading gossip.'

'Oh, I didn't hear it from Megan,' Lauren assured her blithely. 'Lisa Chan told me when I went for my break. Evidently Mick Monaghan had told her.'

Lucy barely managed not to groan. Lisa worked in A and E and Mick was one of the porters! It seemed that the story was gathering momentum fast! She couldn't help wondering what Tom was going to say when it got back to him, as it was bound to do in time. After what had gone on last night, he would probably take a very dim view of people gossiping about them!

'Well, I think it's a shame that people don't have anything better to talk about, quite frankly!' she stated firmly. 'I shall tell you what I told Megan: there is nothing going on between me and Tom Farrell. OK?'

'If you say so,' Lauren agreed, although she didn't sound convinced. She let the subject drop for the rest of their lunch break but Lucy knew that it wasn't the end of it. The rumours were going to keep on circulating unless someone did something to stop them, but what?

She was still mulling it over when she went back to work. Tom was doing a ward round and had stopped to speak to David Blake. He called her over to join them. Rob and Meredith were there as well and she couldn't help noticing how tense the other woman looked. It was obvious that things hadn't been resolved between Meredith and Rob and she made up her mind that she would try to do something about it if she could. She smiled wryly. Not that she could claim to be any sort of expert on relationships, with her track record!

'So, as I was saying, Mr Blake, I'm very pleased with the way things went yesterday,' Tom continued as she hurriedly focused her thoughts on what was happening. 'Jonathan came through the operation extremely well and I'm not anticipating any further problems.'

'Well, that's good to hear.' David Blake glanced at his small son and grimaced. 'Could you just explain to me once again what you did, Dr Farrell? I'm afraid I didn't really take it all in yesterday.'

'That isn't surprising.' Tom glanced at Rob. Lucy saw him frown as he realised that Rob didn't appear to be listening to what was going on. She guessed that Rob was still worrying himself to death over this problem with Meredith but he really needed to concentrate on his work. Although Tom was sympathetic towards his staff, he was so focused himself that he expected the same degree of commitment from those who worked for him. She wasn't surprised to hear the cool note in his voice as he addressed the younger man.

'Perhaps you'd like to take over from here, Dr Turner?'

'Oh...I...er...' Rob stammered. Lucy knew that he hadn't the vaguest idea what he was supposed to be doing and felt so sorry for him that she mouthed instructions. It was just unfortunate that Tom happened to glance round at that moment and saw what she was doing.

She flushed as he gave her a cold stare, knowing in her heart that she had been at fault for interfering even though it had been done with the best of intentions. However, it seemed her efforts to help had only made things worse because his tone was icier than ever as he addressed Rob.

'Perhaps it would help if I repeated what I want you to do, Dr Turner? Would you please explain to Mr Blake exactly what we did yesterday for his son?'

Rob cleared his throat then hurriedly launched into a summary of the previous day's operation. Lucy could tell that he was mortified by the reprimand. He was an excellent doctor and normally gave the job one hundred per cent effort. It just proved that the situation between him and Meredith needed resolving as soon as possible.

'What does it mean exactly when you say that Jonathan had a septal defect?' David Blake asked when Rob had finished. 'I thought he had something wrong with his heart.'

'That's right.' Tom smiled reassuringly. 'A septal defect is just a fancy name for a hole in the heart. In Jonathan's case it wasn't all that big so we were able to close it without too much difficulty. The same goes for the intestinal atresia. We were able to remove the narrowed section of intestine and once things have had time to settle down I'm not anticipating any further problems in that area.'

'Well, that's a relief.' David Blake sounded a lot happier now that he understood what had been done. 'I'll be able to phone Mary and tell her that everything went so well.

She's been so worried, you see, especially as she wasn't able to be here with Jonathan.'

'I'm sure she must have been. Now, is there anything else you'd like to ask me, Mr Blake?' Tom asked, giving the impression that he had all the time in the world to spare.

Lucy knew what a packed schedule he had that day but he gave no sign of it and once again she was struck by his compassion. This wasn't just another case to be written up. Tom really cared about the people he dealt with. She was suddenly proud to be working with him. There were few doctors of his calibre even at Lizzie's, which was renowned for its staff!

'Well…' David Blake hesitated as though he wasn't sure he should mention what was on his mind. 'How bad is Jonathan going to be, Dr Farrell? Oh, I understand that he isn't going to be, well…normal, but will he be able to walk and talk…do things like that?'

Tom sighed. 'I'm afraid I can't give you a definite answer because we don't know yet how severely affected Jonathan is going to be. All I can say is that he will undoubtedly be able to walk and talk, although his progress will probably be slower than that of other children. Down's children are capable of learning and many actually learn to read and write,' he explained carefully.

Lucy realised that he was trying not to downplay the problems of what the future might hold by painting too rosy a picture, but at the same time he wanted to give the parents something to cling to at this very difficult time.

'So it isn't all bad, then?' David Blake exclaimed in relief. 'I wasn't sure what to expect, to be honest. I've heard about Down's syndrome, of course, but you don't take much notice when it doesn't affect you. Still I'll be able to tell Mary all that you've said and I'm sure it will help.' He held out his hand. 'Thank you, Dr Farrell. I really appreciate everything you've done for Jonathan.'

'You're welcome.' Tom shook his hand. 'And if there is

anything else you want to know then please don't hesitate to ask one of the nurses to contact me.'

They left David Blake sitting with his son as they moved to the next incubator which held Liam Mitchell, the baby who had been brought in suffering the effects of drug withdrawal. Tom quickly outlined the case history for everyone's benefit then turned to Lucy and it was impossible not to notice the chill in his voice.

'Have the parents been in to visit him yet, Staff, do you know?'

'Not so far. However, I have warned everyone to be on their guard as you requested, sir,' she replied politely, although it stung to hear him speak to her in that distant manner. Was he still annoyed about her attempts to help Rob out of a tight spot? she wondered. It seemed the most likely explanation. But it made her wonder if it might not be best to make him aware of the problem between Rob and Meredith if it was going to affect their work. She decided to have a word with him later, then focused her attention firmly on what was happening before she earned herself any more black marks!

'I thought chlorpromazine was used to treat babies like this?' Meredith queried as Tom passed her the baby's notes.

'It is. However, in this case I decided that there was no option but to use chloral hydrate and phenobarbitone to control the seizures. It was imperative that we stopped the child having any more because of the long-term damage they could cause,' he explained patiently. He handed the notes back to Lucy when Meredith nodded.

'Thank you, Staff. We shall continue treatment for the next twenty-four hours and then review it.'

Once again there was that same coolness in his voice but she tried to ignore it. There was little she could say with the others there, but once she had chance to explain then she was sure Tom would understand why she had tried to help Rob.

She updated the baby's notes, then slipped them back

into the holder and followed the others to the next incubator. Rob hung back to wait for her and his expression was wry. 'Thanks for trying to help me out before. I'd no idea what I'd been asked to do!'

'I rather gathered that! You were miles away. You and Meredith need to get this sorted out, Rob. Tom won't take kindly to you daydreaming during ward rounds,' she warned.

He grimaced. 'I know! It's just so damned difficult…'

'If you two would care to join us then I'm sure Meredith and I would appreciate it. I would like to get this round over and done with as soon as possible.'

Tom's voice was laced with sarcasm and Lucy flushed as she saw that he was watching them. She hurried over to join him, feeling the shiver which ran down her spine as he gave her a withering look, although she couldn't help feeling that his reaction was rather more than the crime deserved. Could it be that his annoyance stemmed as much from what had happened between them the night before?

It wasn't the most comforting of thoughts, so she put it firmly to the back of her mind and focused on her work. It certainly wouldn't endear her to Tom in his present mood if he caught *her* daydreaming!

The next baby on the list that day was the little girl who had been born as a result of the RTA. She was still hooked up to a vast array of machinery which was monitoring her for cardiorespiratory problems and checking her temperature, blood pressure and oxygen saturation as well. She would need careful monitoring for some time to come but everyone had been surprised by her tenacity as she had clung to life.

The police had launched an appeal asking for any relatives to come forward and one of the newspapers had headed the story with the tag line 'Rosemary's Baby' as that had been her mother's name. Not surprisingly the name had stuck and the nurses had started to call her Rosie.

The story had generated a lot of interest and well-wishers

had sent presents to the hospital for her. Someone had placed a fluffy pink teddy bear at the bottom of her incubator and Lucy smiled as she saw that it was bigger than the baby was. However, day by day she was growing that bit stronger even if there was still a long way to go.

Tom ran through the details once more in his usual thorough way, then set aside the notes and looked at the child. 'My main concern now is the danger of bronchopulmonary dysplasia. It's always a problem with babies who require long-term ventilation like this.'

'What do you think causes it?' Rob asked, his interest obviously piqued. 'I've read a lot about BPD but there seem to be so many theories as to why it occurs and nobody seems to know which one is right.'

Tom nodded. 'I know what you mean. BPD has been attributed to oxygen toxicity, respiratory infection due to intubation, and barotrauma from positive airway pressure ventilation to name just a few. However, I tend to think that it's a combination of many factors which causes the problem, and it is a problem when you consider that sixty per cent of babies who receive artificial ventilation are subsequently readmitted to hospital.'

'So what can we do to minimise the risks?' Meredith asked, frowning. 'I mean, a baby this preterm has to be ventilated and yet it's that which causes the problems later on.'

'It's a fine balance but I think we can achieve a lot by doing exactly what we are at present, i.e. maintain oxygen therapy but use nasal cannulae and low-flow oxygen, and ensure that nutrition is as good as possible to promote adequate lung growth. I'm also a great believer in the use of vitamin E in a case like this, although not everyone agrees with me about that.' He paused thoughtfully. 'If there is a problem weaning the baby off oxygen, then using steroids for a limited period can achieve good results, although that is much in the future in this case.'

'What will happen to her when she leaves here? A baby

like this is going to need an awful lot of care,' Meredith asked with a catch in her voice.

Lucy shot her a quick glance and was surprised to see the glimmer of tears in her eyes. Baby Rosie's story was a touching one but it wasn't like the normally controlled Meredith to be so emotional, unless it was just that her emotions were so topsy-turvy because of what was going on between her and Rob. She sighed as she looked at the baby again. She certainly knew how it felt to be mixed up!

'I'm afraid that is another bridge we shall have to cross when the time comes,' Tom replied sadly. 'If nobody comes forward to claim her then I'm sure that social services will arrange for her to be fostered by someone who understands what they are taking on.'

There wasn't much anyone could add to that. Lucy cast a last look at the child, praying that someone would come forward to claim her. It would be nice to have a happy ending to this very sad tale.

They continued the round but most of the other babies in the unit were well on the road to recovery. Jade Jackson's parents arrived just as they were finishing and Tom stopped to have word with them. Jade would be going home in a few days' time and she knew that they needed reassuring that they would be able to cope.

Taking their child home was a worrying time for parents who had a baby in the intensive care unit. However, they were always offered support from the hospital's home care team and most soon overcame their initial fear and coped wonderfully well. Mr and Mrs Jackson would manage fine and soon enjoy having their precious little daughter at home with them.

Lauren called her over to check on a drip which didn't seem to be flowing as well as it should be. Lucy agreed that it needed changing and sent the younger nurse off to get a replacement. Rob and Meredith had gone over to the door to wait for Tom and she saw Rob say something to her. However, Meredith simply turned on her heel and left the unit without answering him.

She sighed, realising that whatever was wrong must be really serious for Meredith to act this way. She was just wondering what it could be when Tom came over to her.

'Right, Staff, that's it for today. Thank you,' he informed her formally. 'Page me if you need me.'

It was just the opportunity she needed so she jumped straight in. 'Before you go can I have a word with you about Rob—?' she began, but he didn't let her finish.

'I'm afraid I haven't got time to spare at the moment. However, if you would like some good advice then I suggest that you confine your private life to outside working hours.' He gave her a tight smile, ignoring her shocked gasp as she realised that he had misunderstood what she had been trying to say. 'Please don't think that you can play on the fact that we were friends once, Lucy. I expect the same standards from you as I expect from the rest of my team. If you cannot meet them then perhaps it would be best if you thought about a change of direction.'

He turned on his heel and strode out of the room, leaving her reeling. Had Tom *really* said that to her—suggested that she should think about changing her job?

She found it hard to believe and yet she had heard it with her own ears. He hadn't even given her chance to explain what she'd wanted to, which wasn't like him at all. It made her heart ache as she found herself wondering why he should have acted so out of character.

Was he so anxious to get her out of his life after last night that he was using her friendship with Rob as an excuse? Did he feel so guilty about that kiss that he couldn't bear to have her around and be reminded of the lapse he had made?

Painful though it was, it was the only explanation she could come up with. It took her all her time to pretend nothing was wrong when Lauren came back and they set to work changing the drip, but she couldn't close her mind to the thought that Tom didn't want her in his life…in any way!

The afternoon flew past, thankfully enough. Lucy was glad that they were so busy that she didn't have time to brood. Surprisingly, Peter Foster's visit had achieved unexpected results because Emma seemed to accept what had happened at last.

Lucy helped her pack her belongings, then accompanied her downstairs to where a taxi was waiting to take her home. It had been too much to hope that Peter Foster would wait to take Emma home himself, but at least he hadn't made the situation worse by dropping his bombshell about their marriage being over. Maybe he'd had a change of heart, she speculated, mentally crossing her fingers.

She gave the other woman a hug as they said goodbye. 'Take care of yourself, Emma, won't you?'

'I will. Thank you for everything you've done for me and…and Abigail.' Emma blinked back her tears and Lucy squeezed her hand.

'I only wish it could have turned out differently,' she said, sadly. 'but it just wasn't to be.'

'No.' Emma gave her a watery smile then went and got into the waiting cab.

Lucy waved her off, sighing as she went back to the unit. She could only hope that Emma would come to terms with her loss in time, but she couldn't help thinking that it was going to take a long while for her to get over it. She was still thinking about her when she stepped out of the lift and heard a commotion further along the corridor.

She hurried to see what was happening and was met by the sight of Megan physically barring the door to the intensive care unit.

'What's going on?' she demanded as she went to her assistance, shooting a look at the young couple who were causing all the trouble.

'Liam Mitchell's parents,' Megan explained succinctly.

'They say that they want to take him home and that we can't keep him here against their wishes.'

'I see.' Lucy looked at the pair, inwardly sighing as she saw how young they were. They both looked so thin and unkempt that her sympathy was immediately aroused. There were lots of youngsters living rough in London and she guessed that they fell into that category. However, her main concern at that moment had to be the welfare of the baby so she quickly debated calling Security and having them deal with the problem. Yet, if she did that it undoubtedly would lead to them being banned from the hospital. Maybe she could try to make them see that this wasn't the way to go about things?

'I'm Staff Nurse Benson,' she explained, raising her voice to carry over the general hubbub. There were several parents visiting the unit and they were adding their voices to the confusion, plus a couple of the babies had begun crying as well. The last thing she wanted was for already sick babies to become stressed by the amount of noise which was being generated, so she decided that the best thing to do was to get Liam's parents away from the unit.

'I think we need to have a talk. So why don't we go along to the office and—?'

'There's nothing to talk about! We just want our baby back.' The young man stepped forward and glared at her. He was painfully thin, his skin an unhealthy yellowish-white colour, his hair shaved so close to his head that his scalp showed through. He looked very threatening as he towered over her and she had a momentary qualm as she wondered if there was any point trying to reason with him in this mood. However, she refused to back down and stood her ground.

'I understand that. However, there is no way that you can take Liam home at the moment. He is very, very sick and if you remove him from here then the odds are that he will die,' she stated bluntly, deciding that this wasn't the time to skirt around the facts.

'Oh!' The girl pressed a trembling hand to her mouth. She, too, was painfully thin, her long dark hair straggling around her pale face. She couldn't be more than sixteen, by Lucy's estimation, little more than a child herself, in fact. She was obviously very upset by what she had heard so Lucy took the opportunity to try and reason with her.

'What's your name?' she asked in a gentler tone.

'Callie.' The girl ran the back of her hand over her eyes. 'Callie Mitchell.'

'Well, Callie, I think that we all need to sit down and talk about this calmly, don't you? Come along to the office and we'll see what we can sort out.' She glanced at Megan, who didn't look at all happy about the idea.

'Are you sure that's wise, Lucy?' she asked under her breath, shooting a worried glance at the young couple.

'Not really, but I don't want this all spiralling out of control. Can you ask Sandra to lurk round outside the office once you've got things calmed down, in case I need reinforcements?' she suggested with a light laugh, trying to sound more confident than she actually felt. Drug addicts were notoriously difficult to deal with and she had no idea if it was just Liam's mother who was addicted or his father as well.

'Will do.' Megan didn't say anything else but she still didn't look happy as she hurried away.

'This way. The office is just along here.'

Lucy smiled encouragingly at the young couple and after a moment's hesitation they followed her along the corridor. She got them seated then went round the desk, but before she had time to sit down the young man burst out belligerently, 'You can't keep our baby here; it's against the law!'

She gave him a steady look as she sat down, sensing the fear which lurked behind his aggressive attitude. Although it didn't make the situation any the less volatile, it gave her something to focus on. The fact that he cared what happened to the child was an encouraging sign.

'We have a duty to care for any child who is brought into this hospital,' she explained in a deliberately neutral tone. 'To carry out that duty we can ask the local authority to apply to the courts for an emergency protection order. That is what we shall do if you insist on trying to remove Liam against our advice.'

'You can't do that!' The boy burst out, but she could tell that he didn't believe that any more than Callie obviously did. The young girl gave a moan of dismay as tears began streaming down her face.

The boy shot her an anguished look. Lucy guessed that he was at a loss to know what to do. He suddenly slumped forward and put his head in his hands and she could hear the bitterness in his voice.

'I knew this would happen. I knew they'd find some way to take the baby away from us!'

Lucy glanced from him to the girl and her voice softened as she saw the despair on both their faces. It was obvious that they both cared about Liam despite how it might have appeared at first. Maybe there was a way to sort things out after all?

'Is that why you took Liam out of hospital so soon after he was born?' she asked gently.

'Yes.' Callie was twisting a ragged bit of tissue between her thin hands. 'Ben said that they'd take him away because…well, because of me taking drugs.'

She suddenly looked up and Lucy's heart ached as she saw the anguish on her face. 'I did try to stop! Honestly! I went to this doctor and he gave me some stuff…methadone, to stop me wanting the drugs. I had to go to the surgery every day and I did it. When Liam was born there seemed to be nothing wrong with him so I couldn't see any harm in taking him out of the hospital. Ben kept saying that if we weren't careful then social services would take him away and I didn't want that to happen.'

'That's why you gave the hospital a false address, so

nobody could trace you?' Lucy queried and saw the girl grimace.

'Yes. Anyway, we took him back to the squat where we live and he seemed to be fine at first. Oh, he cried a lot and kept wanting to be picked up, but Ben said that all babies do that. Then he started to be sick and couldn't keep his feeds down. And then he had that fit...' Callie broke into a storm of weeping.

Lucy sighed as she passed her a box of tissues. 'Babies born to mothers who have been taking methadone often don't present any symptoms of withdrawal for two to three weeks, which is why Liam appeared well at first. However, he is a very sick little boy and he is going to need a lot of care. This is the best place for him and I'm afraid that you are just going to have to accept that.'

'And after that, then what will happen?' Ben stood up and began pacing the floor. 'They'll take him into care, won't they? Well, I grew up in a home and I hated every minute of it. I don't want my kid being brought up that way!'

He swung round and thumped his fist on the desk to emphasise the point. Lucy could tell that he was becoming very agitated again and tried her best to stay calm. She was suddenly very conscious of how vulnerable she was trapped behind the desk like this.

She glanced towards the door, wondering where Sandra was. However, there was no sign of the other woman so she realised that she had to deal with the situation as best she could by herself.

'Then you have to convince everyone that you are capable of looking after Liam,' she stated in her most matter-of-fact tone, although it was difficult to hide her nervousness.

'Oh, yeah? And you think anyone's going to listen to us? Get real! People like us don't have any rights, understand? We're non-people, we don't exist. How many times have you walked past someone like us huddled up in a doorway and looked the other way?'

Ben laughed scornfully as he leant across the desk and glared at her. 'Who's going to take any notice of what we want, eh?'

CHAPTER EIGHT

'I SHALL, for a start.'

They all froze at the sound of the voice. Lucy felt her heart leap as she looked up and saw Tom in the doorway. She took a deep breath to steady her racing pulse as he came unhurriedly around the desk and stood behind her. She felt his knuckles brush the nape of her neck as he rested his hands on the back of her chair and wondered if he had done it deliberately, before she blanked the thought from her mind. However, it was impossible not to feel reassured as he stood there, so big and solid and dependable. It made her realise just how scared she had been before.

'However, if you want me or anyone else to take account of your wishes then you have to convince us that your main concern is Liam's welfare.' Tom took charge with an easy authority which instantly gained everyone's attention. Lucy found herself thinking how odd it was that he managed to command respect with so little effort. Even Ben seemed to have calmed down now as he sank onto his chair and stared at the floor as Tom continued in the same authoritative tone.

'How are you going to care for him? Where are you going to live? And then there's the issue of your drug-taking to be taken into account.'

He shook his head. 'From where I stand you don't have a lot going for you and if I were a judge then I most certainly wouldn't be in favour of you bringing up a child.'

Ben's face flamed. 'I don't do drugs! I never have. It's a mug's game!'

'I'm glad to hear it. But Callie has been taking them and I know from my own experience of dealing with addicts how difficult it is for them to stop,' Tom said flatly, not giving an inch. Lucy wondered if he wasn't being a little hard on the young couple, but she kept her thoughts to herself.

'I…I want to come off them,' Callie whispered. 'But it isn't easy.'

'That's why you need support.' Tom's tone softened. 'If I could find you a place on a rehabilitation programme, would you take it? You would have to be serious about wanting to stop taking them, though. It isn't something you can do half-heartedly. You need to be really motivated to succeed, but it would be a start and most certainly go in your favour if you want to keep your son.'

'Well…' She hesitated as she looked at Ben. Lucy held her breath. It wasn't just baby Liam's future at stake here but Callie's as well.

Ben reached for her hand. 'You can do it, Callie,' he said gruffly. 'For Liam and me.'

Lucy felt a lump come to her throat as she saw the love in his eyes. Ben so obviously cared that she found herself willing the girl to agree.

Callie took a deep breath before she tossed back her straggling hair. There was a new determination in her eyes, a sense of purpose which had been missing before. 'I…I'll give it a go if you think it will help us keep Liam. I…I don't want to lose him.'

'Good girl!' Tom's delight was obvious as he gave the girl a warm smile. However, Lucy was conscious of how quickly the warmth faded when he turned to her. 'I'll just take them through to see Liam for a few minutes. However, I would like a word with you, Staff, so will you wait here, please? I won't be long.'

'Certainly, Dr Farrell.'

He didn't say anything more before he escorted the young couple from the room. Lucy got up as soon as they'd gone and went to the window to look out across the park. Night was drawing in and she could see her own reflection in the darkened glass. She closed her eyes, not needing to see the shadows in her eyes to know how much it hurt to have Tom treat her so coldly all the time…

'What the hell did you think you were playing at? Have you no sense at all?'

The sound of his angry voice brought her spinning round and she blanched as she saw the expression on his face. He crossed the room in a couple of long strides, catching hold of her by the arms as he gave her a quick shake which made her head spin from the sheer shock of what was happening.

'Didn't you realise what a risk you were taking, bringing them in here by yourself?' he demanded.

'I…I just wanted to get them away from the unit because of the disruption they were causing—' she began hesitantly, but he cut her off angrily.

'That's no excuse! Come on, Lucy, you don't need me to tell you how volatile the situation was!' He glared at her yet beneath the anger she saw real concern in his eyes and her heart began to beat in short, sharp bursts. Tom had been really scared that she might get hurt just now and that was why he was so angry! The thought made her feel breathless and dizzy so that it was hard to think straight.

'I…I suppose it was a silly thing to do, but if I'd called Security then they might have ended up being banned from seeing Liam…' she offered hesitantly, tailing off as she heard him sigh.

'And you wouldn't have wanted that to happen?' He shook his head in exasperation but she could still see the concern in his eyes. 'You always did have a soft heart, Lucy—too soft sometimes.'

'So did you, Tom,' she said quietly. 'Otherwise you wouldn't have offered to help Callie just now.'

He gave a deep laugh which sent a shiver racing down her spine. 'We're a right pair, aren't we?'

He suddenly seemed to realise what he had said because he quickly let her go. Moving away, he sat on the edge of the desk and gave a weary sigh. 'Anyway, we need to work out a plan of action where Liam and his parents are concerned,' he said in a deliberately businesslike tone, although she wasn't deaf to the grating note in his voice.

She took a quick breath but it was impossible to ignore what had happened when once again she found her emotions see-sawing back and forth. Tom had said that he wanted to forget the past but it was hard to do that when even a chance remark brought everything back. Did he find it as difficult as she did to separate his feelings? Or was he able to put them into nice tidy compartments...one place for what had happened five years ago, another for what was happening now? From what he had said she doubted it and she couldn't stop her heart from beating that bit faster at the thought. No matter how Tom might want to erase the memory of their past, it just wasn't possible! It was an effort to concentrate as he continued in the same no-nonsense tone.

'Ben and Callie are not to be left alone with Liam at any time. Whenever they visit I want either a member of staff or a security officer to be present,' he explained firmly.

'I understand.' She took a quick breath as she heard the huskiness in her voice. 'About what you told Callie—do you think you can get her a place on a rehabilitation course?'

'It won't be easy because there are always more youngsters needing help than there are places available. However, I did some work with the drug rehabilitation team in Cornwall so I do have a few contacts. I'll see if I can call in a few favours. Whether she'll stick it out is anyone's guess. You know as well as I do how many addicts drop out before they complete the course. And then there is the temptation to go back on drugs once they return to their former lives.'

'But she has Ben and the baby to think about,' Lucy declared. 'They are the best incentive in the world for her to beat the habit!'

He shrugged. 'Maybe. But it isn't going to be easy for

her and we mustn't kid ourselves that everything is all cut and dried just because she has agreed to give it a try.'

'But we have to give her the benefit of the doubt, Tom!' she countered fiercely. 'We have to believe that she can do it, otherwise she won't stand a chance.'

He gave her a lopsided grin, the dimple flashing in his lean cheek. 'Ever the optimist, Lucy. You always refused to give up and admit that things might not work out how you wanted them to.'

She felt a lump come to her throat and looked away in case he saw the anguish in her eyes. She'd given up on them *and* been forced to admit that there was no way forward for their relationship when it would have meant denying Tom something he had wanted so much! Yet the pain she felt even now about what she'd had to do was so fierce that it made her heart ache.

Why did it still hurt so much? she found herself wondering. Why hadn't five years dimmed the anguish? The answer was there at the very back of her mind but something warned her that it would be a mistake to look too hard for it.

Tom sighed when she didn't answer. Whether he thought her silence strange she had no idea but, thankfully, his pager sounded at that moment. He checked the display, then got up.

'I have to go. Are you sure you're all right? I know you had a bit of a scare just now…'

'I'm fine. Really.' She gave him a bright smile, praying that he couldn't tell how her heart was aching. 'Don't worry about me, Tom.'

'Well, if you're sure…' He hesitated, then gave her a quick smile and hurried from the room.

She took a deep breath, closing her mind to everything else but the practicalities of getting through the rest of the day. There was no point in wishing for things which couldn't happen or regretting what had been done. It was the here and now which mattered, what happened today and tomorrow and all the rest of the days of her life. Suddenly they seemed to spread before her, empty and lonely without Tom to fill them…

The next few days passed uneventfully but she was glad when the shift came to an end. It just so happened that her days off fell at a weekend so she debated going to see her sister to get away for a while. She had been working all over Christmas so hadn't been able to go then and it had been some while since she had seen her. However, when she rang Cathy on the Friday night it was to learn that the family was heading off to stay with friends for the weekend. It left her out on a limb for the next three days.

On Saturday morning, in an effort to stave off an impending case of the blues, she took the bus to Oxford Street and did some window shopping, but even the shops held little appeal. It was the end of the January sales and everywhere had that dreary, post-sales look. She spent barely an hour there then, thankfully, headed away from the hustle and bustle, letting her feet take her where they would, and ended up in Regent's Park, close to the hospital. It seemed she couldn't stay away from the place!

It was a cold, crisp day, a milky sun taking the worst of the chill out of the air. There were a few brave souls out jogging and a few more walking their dogs. She followed the path around the lake, suddenly glad to be out in the fresh air.

She came to the end of the path and debated which way to go next. Ahead of her was the children's playground and to her right a small bridge leading towards the centre of the park. She decided to go that way and head towards the zoo instead of going home. The thought of being on her own in the flat didn't appeal. The silence only served to remind her of how empty her life was. Oh, she had her work, and she enjoyed it, but she knew that it wasn't enough to take the place of a loving relationship. Funny, but she'd been quite happy until Tom had come back into her life, but his return had stirred up all sorts of feelings she had long since relegated to the past.

She was just thinking about how mixed up she had felt recently when she noticed the man and child on the far side of the bridge and her heart leapt as she realised that it was Tom and Adam. She came to a halt, wondering whether it would be best to turn back before they saw her. However, just at that moment Adam spotted her.

'Lucy!' He shouted in delight as he came racing towards her. 'Daddy and me have got bread for the ducks,' he informed her importantly, holding out a crumpled paper bag full of crusts for her inspection.

'How lovely! I bet they're really glad that you've brought them something nice to eat,' she replied, laughing at his excitement and thinking how adorable he looked in his bright red bobble hat and matching jacket.

'Hello, Lucy. Have you come to feed the ducks as well?'

There was a teasing warmth in Tom's voice as he came to join them which sent a ripple of pleasure through her as soon as she heard it. She took a quick breath to still her madly beating heart, thinking how *adorable* he looked as well in a blue quilted jacket and jeans, his feet laced into sturdy leather boots. The outfit gave him an unfamiliarly rugged appearance and she felt her pulse race like crazy as she saw how attractive he looked. It was an effort to keep her tone light so that he wouldn't guess the effect he was having on her!

'I never thought to bring any bread with me, I'm afraid. I wish I had done now. It looks like fun.'

'Here.' Adam delved into the bag and handed her a crumbling crust. 'Now you can feed the ducks!'

Tom laughed softly. 'Problem solved. Come along, then, we have a lot of hungry mouths to feed.'

He led the way back to the bridge and after a moment's hesitation she followed him. After all, what could be more innocent then feeding the ducks? she reasoned. However, it was hard to ignore the rapid beating of her heart as she broke off a piece of crust and tossed it into the water and she sighed inwardly. Who was she trying to fool? Just being with Tom was enough to turn even something as innocuous as this into an event of some importance!

'There, Daddy…that brown one. He hasn't had any.' Adam claimed her attention and she smiled as she saw the concern on his face as he pointed out a small duck standing on its own halfway up the banking. He looked so like Tom with that frown on his face that it made her wonder if he had inherited Tom's compassionate nature as well.

'Which one?' Tom queried, frowning as he looked at the crowd of ducks which were milling around.

'Over there…see, by that bush.' She touched his arm to point out where to throw the bread and he grinned at her.

'How on earth can you recognise one duck from another?' he teased.

She laughed at that. 'I can't, but Adam can! If he says that one hasn't had any bread, then I'm sure he's right.'

Tom rolled his eyes. 'Well, I suppose I shall just have to believe you, but I'm not convinced.' He tossed a piece of bread onto the banking, laughing as Adam clapped his hands in delight as the little duck gobbled it up. They carried on until all the bread had gone and the last crumbs had been emptied out of the paper bag.

Tom rolled the bag into a ball and stuffed it into his pocket, then looked at his son. 'Right, then. Where to now?'

'Swings!' Adam shouted, racing back across the bridge in the direction of the playground.

Tom shook his head. 'I don't know where he gets his energy from! Would you believe that I was sitting up in bed reading to him at six o'clock this morning?' He groaned but Lucy could tell that he didn't really mind. 'I ended up playing monsters with him just so that I could snatch a few extra minutes' sleep.'

'Sounds a good game to me.' She laughed. 'How do you play it?'

'Well, you begin with everyone snuggling down beneath the duvet and listening in case you can hear a monster creeping along the hall.' Tom was having trouble keeping his face straight. 'Of course, you have to be very, very quiet and you might need to listen for quite a long time...'

'And while Adam was doing that, being quiet and listening, you were fast asleep?' She laughed out loud. 'I never thought you could be so devious, Tom!'

He grinned as they followed Adam across the bridge. 'It isn't devious, it's a simple matter of survival. You find that you develop previously unknown talents when you have a child like Adam. He was one of those awful babies who don't believe in sleeping for very long in case they miss something. He's a lot better now, thank heavens, but I learned early on to snatch forty winks whenever I got the chance otherwise I wouldn't have been fit for anything!'

Lucy laughed at that, although she couldn't help feeling rather puzzled. He made it sound as though he had borne the brunt of looking after Adam when he was a baby. It made her wonder why Fiona hadn't taken more of a share in it. Surely it would have made sense if Tom had needed to get up for work?

It was on the tip of her tongue to ask him when she realised that he would only think it impertinent of her to ask such questions. She sighed, wondering why she found the thought of Tom sharing his life with the other woman so painful. Every time the thought crossed her mind it seemed to leave another little scar on her heart.

They had reached the playground by then and she paused uncertainly, wondering if it was wise to spend any more time in his company. Being around Tom was never easy, and especially not when he was in this sort of relaxed mood. It was only too easy to forget what had happened and what a gulf there really was between them, but she knew deep down how dangerous it was. She and Tom simply weren't the same two people they had been five years ago and the proof of that was Adam!

He looked round as he realised that she had stopped. 'Aren't you coming in?'

'Well, I'm not sure,' she began, frantically searching for an excuse which sounded plausible.

'Come on, Lucy, it will do you good to get some fresh air after being cooped up in work all week,' he said persuasively. He looked at the sky and grimaced. 'The weather forecast said that we should expect snow in the next few days so this might be your last chance.'

She frowned. 'I don't recall hearing that?'

'No?' He gave her an innocent smile. 'Oh, well, I was half asleep when the bulletin came on the radio…'

'*And* probably had your head under the duvet,' she finished for him, chuckling.

'Something like that!' he agreed, laughing. He sobered all of a sudden. 'OK, you caught me out, I've no idea what the forecast was, but please say that you'll stay a bit longer. I could do with the company, to be honest. Much as I love Adam, sometimes it can be, well…rather lonely, just the two of us.'

The quiet confession touched her heart so that it took a moment before she was sure there was no trace of emotion in her voice. Tom obviously misunderstood her silence.

'Sorry. It's not fair to go dumping my problems on you.' He gave her a quick smile but she could see the bleakness in his eyes. 'I expect you've got lots of things to do without us taking up any more of your time.'

She shook her head, suddenly finding it impossible to lie. 'I haven't. In fact, I can't think of anything I would enjoy more than spending some time with you and Adam, if you want me to.'

'Sure?' He still sounded doubtful so she hurried to convince him.

'Positive!'

He grinned. 'Great! So what are we waiting for?'

He pushed open the small iron gate leading into the playground for her. Adam was by the climbing frame so she hurried over to him although she couldn't help wondering if she was doing the right thing. Maybe Tom did feel lonely at the moment but it was understandable. It must be a big change for him coming to live in London, away from all his friends. However, he would soon make new friends and then where would that leave her? Wasn't it simply inviting more heartache to let herself get too involved?

She closed her mind to the nagging voice of reason because she didn't want to hear what it had to say. She wanted to spend time with him and Adam whether it was sensible or not!

They played in the park for over an hour before the chill of the afternoon finally drove them to seek shelter. The sun was starting to slip from the sky and the air was turning frosty. Lucy couldn't remember when she'd last had so much fun and knew that the memory of this afternoon would linger in her mind for a long time to come. Maybe that was why she was so reluctant for it to end.

'How would you both like to come home with me for tea?' she asked impulsively as they headed for the exit. 'We could catch the bus from the end of the road here and it only takes about thirty minutes or so.'

'Sounds like an offer we can't refuse, don't you think, Adam?' Tom grinned as the child began jumping up and down with excitement. His eyes were a warm soft grey as he looked at her. 'Thanks, Lucy, we'd love to come if you're sure we won't be putting you out?'

'Of course not!' she declared, turning away as she felt her heart begin to race. When he looked at her that way it was hard not to think of all the other times she had seen that warmth in his eyes. But that had been a long time ago, she reminded herself sternly. And the situation had changed greatly since those days! Tom certainly wasn't in love with her as he had been back then.

It was just the dampener she needed to set her back on even keel. They left the park and headed for the bus stop and, as luck would have it, one came as soon as they got there. Adam was barely able to contain his excitement as Tom helped him climb the steep stairs to the top deck. Lucy sat him on her knee and pointed out things for him to see along the route: the park where they had just been playing, the huge gold dome of the Central London Mosque with its crescent moon on top, the roof of the hospital just visible through the trees.

Tom stayed silent as she and Adam chattered away, although there was a strange expression on his face when she happened to glance at him. It made her wonder fleetingly if he would have liked to show Adam those things himself, and maybe felt that she was usurping his place, only he didn't appear upset.

She pushed the thought to the back of her mind, realising that she was falling into the trap of trying to work out what he was thinking once again. For this one afternoon at least she would take things at face value and not go looking for ulterior motives!

It was only a five-minute walk to her flat when they got off the bus. She led the way down the basement steps to the front door, wondering what Tom would think of her home as she ushered him and Adam inside. She had worked hard to make the place look cosy, painting the walls a soft peach to counteract the drab green carpet she had inherited from a previous tenant and which she hadn't been able to afford to replace.

The suite was an old cane one she had found in a street market, but she had re-varnished the frame and made new peach floral covers for the cushions, used the same fabric for the simple curtains which draped the window. All in all, it didn't look too bad, she decided critically, but she held her breath as Tom took a long look round.

'It's lovely, Lucy.' He turned to her and smiled warmly. 'You have a real gift for making a place look like home.'

'Th...thank you.' She turned away before he could see how touched she was by the compliment. Why it should matter what he thought of her home was beyond her, but she knew that it did. She quickly headed for the tiny kitchen, speaking over her shoulder because she wasn't sure that her face wouldn't give her away even then.

'Take your coats off, both of you, and make yourself comfortable while I put the kettle on.'

It took her a little while to prepare the tea. She made sandwiches and buttered scones, then sliced a sponge cake she had baked earlier in the week. She enjoyed cooking but it was rare that she invited anyone round so she decided to make the most of the occasion.

Tom had switched on the small portable television when she went back with the tray so that Adam could watch a cartoon programme. He got up as soon as he saw her, hurriedly crossing the room to take the heavy tray from her.

'You should have called me,' he admonished, looking round for somewhere to put it.

'It was fine,' she assured him, warmed by his concern. It was nice to feel cared for because it was such a long time since it had happened. Living on her own, she had grown used to fending for herself, but that didn't mean she didn't appreciate small courtesies like this.

She gave Tom a quick smile as she pointed to the small dining table by the window. 'Perhaps it would be better to put it over there out of the way. I don't want Adam upsetting the teapot on himself.'

'Right.' He set the tray down and began unloading the plates, groaning as he saw the cake. 'Home baked? Oh, I can't tell you how long it's been since I tasted a cake that hasn't come out of a box!'

'Well, you don't need to be polite! Tuck in,' she replied, laughing at his expression. He didn't need telling twice and helped himself to sandwiches and cake, then poured them both tea from the big earthenware pot. Lucy filled a plate for Adam and took it over to him, setting it down beside him on the rug. He was completely absorbed by the cartoon characters' antics and barely took his eyes off the screen to mutter a quick thank you.

'He loves cartoons,' Tom observed ruefully as she sat down.

'Mmm, I wonder who he gets that from?' she teased. 'Somebody not a million miles from here used to be a huge fan, too, as I recall.'

'I can't imagine who you mean,' he said loftily, his eyes dancing with amusement.

'Oh, no?' She put her cup down and glared at him. 'I don't know how you can sit there and say that, Tom Farrell! Would you like me to list all your favourite cartoon characters…?'

'OK! OK! I'll hold my hands up and admit it.' He grinned as he helped himself to a scone. 'I did watch the odd cartoon from time to time.'

She snorted with a sad lack of ladylike grace. 'From time to time is an understatement! Why, I can remember one Saturday morning going on relief to Children's Medical and finding you and a crowd of kids all glued to the set!'

'Mmm, I remember that. Your face was a picture, as I recall. You weren't sure whether you should laugh or tell me off for wasting valuable time,' he retorted, knowing that she hadn't been in a position to reprimand him. He suddenly sighed. 'However, there was an ulterior motive to me sitting with the kids that day. Do you remember Jason Fisher who was in the ward at the time?'

She frowned as she tried to recall the child in question. 'I'm not sure… Oh, not that little boy who had been beaten by his stepfather?'

'That's the one.' His tone was grim all of a sudden. 'The boy was brought in with multiple bruises and lacerations, plus a fractured wrist. He wouldn't say who had done it to him although, according to the mother, it had been a couple of older boys who had set on him. It just didn't ring true to me. There was something about the way Jason acted when his stepfather came in to see him…'

He sighed. 'Anyway, I wanted to get the truth out of him

because I had my suspicions, but the poor kid was so afraid that he didn't trust anyone.'

'So you tried to gain his confidence by spending time with him, watching television and playing games, even telling those deplorable jokes?' Lucy guessed, wondering why she had never realised that before. It had been well-known how much of his own time Tom had spent on the children's wards but she had never understood before why he had done it.

'Uh-huh. With adults it's a lot easier, you can reassure them more often than not simply by explaining the facts, but it's different with children. You need to build up a rapport before they really open up to you.' He stared down at his cup and his face was pensive. 'I needed to get Jason to trust me enough to tell me what had gone on and in the end he did. The sad thing was that he hadn't felt able to tell his mother because he'd been afraid that she wouldn't believe him.'

'I expect the stepfather had made him think that,' she said sadly.

'How did you guess?' His expression was wry. 'Anyway, once the poor kid had admitted who had beaten him up, then I told his mother. She was stunned because she'd had no idea what had been going on. Evidently, she worked long hours, leaving Jason in the stepfather's care, and that's when the incidents happened.'

'So it wasn't just a one-off?' Lucy queried.

''Fraid not. Anyway, the upshot of it all was that the mother threw the stepfather out and the police prosecuted him. The next time I saw Jason for a check-up he looked like a different child. He'd also started to catch up at school because his work had been suffering.'

He leant back in his chair and grinned, making an obvious effort to lighten the sombre mood. 'And all that was thanks to a few cartoons, so don't knock them!'

She laughed as he'd intended but that didn't stop her thinking how lucky Jason Fisher had been to have been

treated by Tom. If it hadn't been for his concern and determination to get to the bottom of the child's problem, then
the situation might not have had such a happy ending.

A shiver ran down her spine at the thought of what might
have happened and she quickly picked up her cup, not
wanting to dwell on it. However, it wasn't easy to dismiss
the fact that her admiration for Tom had simply increased
after hearing that tale. He was so kind and caring that he
seemed to stand head and shoulders above everyone else
she knew. But then he had always been very special to her,
the only man she would ever love.

The thought slid into her mind with little fanfare, but
then it had been only waiting for the chance to do so for
some time. Ever since Tom had come back into her life it
had been hovering on the brink of her consciousness. Now
as she watched him get up and go over to Adam she felt a
wave of relief at being able to admit it to herself at last.

She loved Tom! She had never stopped loving him. It
made sense out of all the confusion, made her understand
why she had felt so mixed up. Even though he might never
be able to return her love, she didn't regret it.

'I'm afraid your carpet is full of crumbs, but obviously
Adam enjoyed the cake as much as I did, from the look of
him!'

The amusement in his voice drew her attention and she
took a small breath before she looked at him. She didn't
want him guessing how she felt because it would be a bur-
den to him. Tom didn't love her and she wouldn't embarrass him by letting him know how she felt.

'A few crumbs don't matter in the least,' she assured
him, summoning a smile. She got up to fetch Adam's plate,
chuckling as she saw that the child's mouth was rimmed
with jam. 'And a drop of soap and water will soon sort out
the rest of the damage! Come along, young man, time for
the bathroom, I think.'

She held out her hand, grimacing as Adam put his sticky
fingers into hers. He giggled happily, realising that she was

teasing him. Tom laughed as he took Adam's dishes to the table and began loading everything onto the tray. 'While you two are ungluing yourselves I'll make a start on washing these—'

He broke off as his pager beeped, sighing as he checked its display. 'The hospital. Can I use your phone, Lucy?'

'Of course. It's over there on the bookcase.' She left him to make the call while she dealt with Adam. She was just drying the child's hands when Tom came to find her.

'Problems?' she guessed, seeing the frown on his face.

'Yes. I wasn't supposed to be on call this weekend, but Jim Bates is anxious about a new admission they've had. Evidently, the child is three weeks old and was being flown back to Italy with her parents when she was taken ill on the plane. They diverted to Heathrow and brought her straight to Lizzie's,' he explained, shooting an anxious look at Adam.

'Don't worry about Adam,' she assured him quickly, realising immediately what the problem was. 'I'll look after him.'

'Are you sure? It doesn't seem fair to keep expecting you to jump in each time there's an emergency, Lucy,' he replied, obviously troubled by the thought of having to accept her help again. 'I could have dropped him off at the crèche only it's a bit late for that now. I've no idea how long I'm going to be.'

She shrugged as Adam ran back into the living room. 'Then it's me or nobody, Tom,' she said lightly, trying not to show how hurt she felt by his reluctance to take her up on her offer.

'Hey, I didn't mean that!' he said quickly, stepping forward to catch hold of her hands. He bent to look into her face and it was impossible not to see that he meant every word. 'I can think of no one I trust more to take care of Adam. It's just that I don't want you thinking that I'm...well, taking advantage of your kindness.'

'Of...of course I don't think that,' she assured him

huskily. She looked away because it was impossible to look into those warm grey eyes and not let him see how she felt. Loving Tom and not being able to show him how she felt was the sweetest kind of torment imaginable.

It was an effort to keep her tone light. 'I enjoy looking after him, Tom, so you are not taking advantage of me.'

He gave her fingers a gentle squeeze, then let her go. 'Then thank you very much for the offer and I shall be happy to accept it. Now to practicalities.' He checked his watch, giving her a few valuable seconds to gather her composure. 'I think it would be better if I called a cab and dropped you and Adam at the flat. He usually goes to bed by seven, you see, so it would be easier if we stuck to his normal routine, if you don't mind, Lucy?'

'Of course not,' she assured him, adopting the same practical tone because it was best. 'I'll just get my things while you ring for a taxi.'

She collected her coat then got Adam ready. He was very excited at the prospect of her going home with them so that it took her all her time to get him zipped into his jacket. The taxi arrived a few minutes later and it seemed to take no time at all before they were drawing up outside the flats.

Tom asked the driver to wait, then saw them safely inside. 'I hate running off and leaving you like this. I haven't even had chance to show you where everything is.'

'Don't worry. Adam and I will manage, won't we, poppet?' She tweaked the pompom on the top of the child's woolly hat as Tom unlocked the door. 'You can show me where everything is while Daddy goes to see the sick baby, can't you?'

Adam nodded importantly. He appeared totally unconcerned by the thought of Tom leaving them as he raced inside. Tom gave her a grateful smile.

'Thanks, Lucy. I can't tell you what a relief this is.'

'It's my pleasure,' she assured him. 'Now, off you go. Adam and I will be fine.'

He hesitated as though he was going to say something.

The oddest expression crossed his face before he suddenly bent and brushed her mouth with a kiss. It was all over almost before she had time to realise what was happening. Tom drew back and smiled at her, his grey eyes tender as he saw the surprise on her face.

'I'll be back as soon as I can,' he said huskily, then turned and hurried away.

Lucy took a quick breath but it did little to ease the constriction in her chest and nothing at all to still the pounding of her heart. Her feet didn't seem to touch the floor as she went inside and got Adam ready for his bath. It made no difference that the voice of reason was whispering that she was letting her imagination run away with her. Her foolish heart had gone strategically deaf. It didn't want to hear any logical reasons why Tom had kissed her. If there were rational explanations then it most certainly didn't want to listen to them. It was happy to cling to the thought that he had kissed her because he had wanted to.

It was the simplest answer in the world and yet the most complex!

CHAPTER NINE

ADAM was more than ready for bed by the time seven o'clock came around. Lucy read him a story but his eyes were closing before she came to the last page. He gave her a sleepy smile as she tucked him up and kissed him good-night. He was fast asleep before she had made it out of the room.

She went into the lounge to wait for Tom to get home. There wasn't anything worth watching on the television so she switched on the stereo instead, hunting through the discs until she came to the one Tom had played for her the last time she'd been there. She fed it into the machine, then curled up on the sofa and settled down to listen. Whether it was the fresh air or the soothing music she didn't know, but she soon fell fast asleep herself and when she awoke Tom was home.

'How long have you been back?' she asked, feeling completely disorientated to see him there. She pushed a silky wisp of hair back from her face, feeling the heat flowing under her skin as she recalled what she had been dreaming about just moments before. It was hard to behave naturally when all she could think about were the images which had filled her head: images of her and Tom…together…

'Oh, only a few minutes,' he assured her although she wasn't sure whether to believe him. He looked very comfortable as he sat sprawled in the armchair, his feet resting on the coffee-table. She had the impression that he had been there for some time and she went hot and cold at the thought of him watching her while she had dreamt those very sexy dreams!

She swung her feet to the floor, deeply unsettled by the

thought. 'Well, you should have woken me,' she admonished.

He shrugged but there was a gleam in his eyes which made her heart race as she saw it. Surely he hadn't guessed what she had been dreaming about?

'Oh, I was going to. I just couldn't decide whether I should do it the tried and tested way, that's all.'

'The tried and tested way?' she repeated blankly, struggling to get a grip on herself.

'Uh-huh. You were always so difficult to wake up, Lucy, that I formulated my own method of getting you up of a morning.' He gave a deep chuckle as he saw her blush. 'I see you remember?'

Of course she remembered! How many times had she woken to the feel of Tom's mouth on hers? It was impossible to count but she could recall how it had felt. His lips had been gentle at first as they had coaxed a response from hers, then they had grown more demanding...

She scrambled to her feet, not wanting to let her mind go any further. Maybe Tom could treat it as a joke, but she couldn't. It just went to prove how different their views were. Things which meant so much to her obviously meant little to him otherwise he couldn't have treated them so lightly!

'What's the matter?' he asked, his smile fading as he saw the expression on her face.

'Nothing,' she replied shortly, looking round and trying to remember where she had put her bag.

'Of course something is wrong!' He frowned as he stood up. 'I was only joking just now.'

'I know you were! I'm glad that you find it all so...so amusing!' she shot back, then wished she hadn't said that as she saw his face darken. What was the point of making an issue out of this? It would only lead to questions about why she was so upset and she most certainly didn't want to go into the ins and outs of that!

She finally spotted her bag under the coffee-table and

bent down to retrieve it, but he caught hold of her arm. His eyes shimmered with puzzlement as he drew her upright. 'Look, Lucy, whatever I've done to upset you I apologise for it. You never used to be so…well, so touchy.'

'I never used to be a lot of things!' She gave a brittle laugh. 'Forget it, Tom. You and I simply have a different view of past events, that's all. I don't suppose it's any wonder really. After all, the time we spent together can't possibly compare to what came after for you.'

'You mean my marriage to Fiona?' His voice was so harsh all of a sudden that she blinked. She stared at him in confusion, watching the rapid play of emotions which crossed his face without understanding half of what she was seeing.

He uttered something rough as he swung round and went to the window. Lucy was at a loss to know what to do. Was he angry about what she had said? And yet there was something about the way he stood there with his head bowed which didn't give her that impression. She was still trying to work out what to do when he suddenly spoke.

'Well, you're right about that. Our time together was nothing like the time I spent married to Fiona. That was a nightmare from start to finish, if you really want to know,' he stated bluntly, seemingly oblivious to her shocked gasp. 'Maybe it was to be expected because neither of us went into it for the right reasons.'

He looked round and his face was all hard angles in the light from the table lamp. 'Does that surprise you, Lucy? After all, you seem to have got it into your head that it was the love match of the decade, but I assure you it wasn't remotely like that.'

'Then why…why did you marry her?' she whispered, struggling to make sense of what he was saying.

'Why do you think?' He laughed hoarsely. 'When you left me I didn't know what had hit me. I was a complete and total mess, to be frank. I met Fiona at a particularly low point and we went out together a few times. She had just come out of a traumatic relationship herself and I think it was a case of us crying on each other's shoulders. It would have been OK if we'd left it at that but somehow we convinced ourselves that we should get married because we had so much in common.'

He shrugged but she could see the regret on his face. 'We realised almost immediately that we'd made a mistake but we hung on, hoping, I suppose, that things would get better once we had time to adjust.'

'B...but they didn't?' she queried, reeling from what he had said. That she had been so wrong about his marriage stunned her so that she found it difficult to concentrate as he continued in the same bitter tone.

'How did you guess? The problem with any relationship is that you can't put into it what isn't there. I didn't love Fiona and she didn't love me. We were on the brink of calling it a day when she discovered that she was pregnant. That changed everything.'

He ran his hand through his hair and his expression was so bleak that she ached to go to him. But what comfort could she offer him when it had been she who had caused this problem in the first place? If she hadn't told him that lie then he would never have married Fiona, never have gone through all the pain and heartache.

'Didn't that help to bring you closer?' she suggested softly, clinging to that hope because it was all she had to stave off her own sense of guilt. 'People say that having a child often helps a marriage.'

'Maybe it does in some cases, but it didn't work for us. Fiona had a difficult pregnancy and hated every moment of it. It simply drove us even further apart. By the time Adam was three months old she had made it clear that she wanted out of the marriage.'

He sighed as he went and sat down. He stared at the floor so that she could no longer see his face clearly, but she could hear the pain in his voice and that was more than enough to know what he was going through.

'I persuaded her to give it another shot because I didn't want to lose Adam, basically. We came back to England and for a time it seemed that things might resolve themselves. Fiona seemed a lot happier, although she took less and less interest in Adam. I didn't want to rock the boat so I didn't say anything. I suppose I was still clinging to the hope that things would work out, if not for our benefit then for Adam's.'

He suddenly looked up and her heart ached at the anguish she saw in his eyes. 'More fool me. It turned out that she had met up with her former fiancé again and they were planning a new life together. Adam definitely didn't feature in it.'

'You're saying that Fiona would have left him behind?' She could hear the incredulity in her own voice and saw him smile thinly.

'I don't think Fiona wanted any reminders of our time together and that included Adam,' he stated bluntly. 'Anyway, the day she was killed she was with him, the boyfriend. I don't really know what went on, whether they had some sort of a row maybe, but Fiona rushed out of the house, leaving Adam asleep. Their car was hit by a tanker about a mile away from where we lived and they were both killed outright.

'It was only later that I was able to piece things together and discovered that Fiona had spent all our savings buying expensive presents for this guy, including the car he was driving when the accident happened. Not a pretty tale, is it? And most certainly not a time I look back on with any great fondness.'

She couldn't stop the tears from flowing down her cheeks. 'Oh, Tom, I had no idea. If only…' She stopped abruptly but he knew what she'd been going to say.

'If only you hadn't left me then none of this would have happened?' He shrugged but it didn't disguise the pain in his eyes, the regret which told her he blamed himself more than Fiona for what had happened. 'But then I wouldn't have Adam, would I? And I can't imagine what my life would be like without him now.'

'No. He…he's the one good thing to come out of all this,' she whispered, knowing that Tom had no idea just how true that was. If they hadn't parted then he wouldn't have met Fiona and had his son, the child that she could *never* have given him. Odd how something so wonderful could come out of so much heartache.

She turned away, almost blinded by tears as she picked up her bag. Any hopes she'd had that Tom might have been able to forgive her in time had disappeared completely now. How could he forgive her for all the pain his marriage had caused him as well as everything else? He was just a man, not superhuman; he felt all the range of emotions from love to hatred. She didn't dare think how he felt about her!

'I'll call you a cab,' he offered, getting up, but she shook her head. She couldn't bear to remain in the flat waiting for it to arrive. She just wanted to go home and close the door on tonight and everything she had learned, but would that be possible? How could she come to terms with the thought that she had caused the man she loved so much pain?

'There's no need,' she assured him, avoiding his eyes in case he saw her anguish. 'I can catch a bus at the end of the road.'

'Sure?' He queried but he didn't pursue it when she nodded. The night was cold as she left the flats but she barely noticed the nip of frosty air as hot tears ran down her face. The funny thing was that she wasn't sure who she was crying for—Tom, for what he had been through, or herself because on the day she had realised how much she still loved him she had also discovered how pointless it was. If Tom had never met her, then his life could have been so much better. How that hurt!

'Right, so how many tickets do we need, then? Sandra, Lauren, me…that's three.' Megan winked at the others then turned to Lucy with an innocent smile. 'Do you want me to get one for you as well, or is someone taking you?'

'Sorry?' She looked up as Lauren chuckled, suddenly realising that all eyes were on her. That she hadn't heard a word of the conversation was clear to all of them and Megan sighed wearily.

'We were talking about the Valentine's Day dance. The poster went up this morning and we need to get the tickets before they all sell out. You're miles away today, Lucy. Whatever is the matter with you? Or should I guess?' Megan grinned wickedly. 'It couldn't be a bad case of *lurv*, could it?'

Everyone laughed at that. Lucy tried her best to smile but inside her heart was aching. She had spent the past two days trying to put what Tom had told her into perspective but she had accomplished very little. Even now that she was back on duty she kept finding her thoughts going back to what she had learned. The worst thing was that she blamed herself for what had happened to him, even though she knew it was foolish.

'I doubt it,' she replied, doing her best to disguise how she felt. 'You know me, "Love 'em and leave 'em" Lucy! There's always a bigger fish in the pond, isn't there?'

She expected everyone to laugh but, surprisingly, the other three looked rather uncomfortable. However, it was only when she heard a familiar voice that she realised why.

'Good morning, everyone.'

Her face flamed as she turned and saw Tom. She couldn't help wondering what he must be thinking but he gave no sign that he had overheard their conversation.

'I'd like to take a look at Lucia Alesi, if you wouldn't mind, Staff,' he said blandly. He turned to Rob and Meredith and she took the opportunity to get herself under control as the other nurses hurried away.

'The Alesi baby was rushed into hospital at the weekend,' he explained. 'According to the mother, the birth was straightforward and there were no complications. However, the child has been difficult to feed and she hasn't been gaining weight. The parents took medical advice but she was passed as fit to fly home to Italy from Dublin, where Mr Alesi has been working. Unfortunately, almost as soon as the plane was airborne it became obvious that there was a problem so the flight was diverted to Heathrow and she was rushed straight here.'

He led the way to the baby's crib. Tiny Lucia had been isolated in a side room and they all donned masks and gowns before entering. He frowned as they gathered around the cot. 'When I examined her on Saturday evening I discovered that she had a rash, which is why I decided to have her isolated. I ordered a full range of tests and the results show abnormal haematological values for her age group. She is neutropenic.'

'So there is a problem with her immune system?' Rob queried thoughtfully. 'How bad is it?'

'That is something we need to determine in the next few days. Hopefully, we won't discover deficiencies with both her T-cells and B-cells. That is the worst-case scenario, of course,' Tom replied.

'SCIDS, severe combined immune deficiency syndrome,' Meredith murmured. 'I remember watching a programme on television years ago about a child who was suffering from that. The poor little mite had spent all his life in isolation because of the risk of him contracting any kind of infection.'

Tom nodded. 'They used to call them "Bubble Babies" because they lived in specially sealed Perspex units. Anyone visiting them—nurses, parents, whoever—had to wear special suits like astronauts wear. Thankfully, we've made some progress since those days and most SCIDS children can be treated in hospital units where the air is constantly reprocessed and purified.'

'How many can be treated with bone marrow transplants?' Rob asked.

'Roughly forty per cent.' Tom sighed. 'Obviously, it's

finding a good match which is always the difficult part. However, it's a long process and the parents need to be very dedicated to ensure it's successful because of the ever-present risk of infection. Until we get all the test results back, we shall have to assume the worst and keep the child in strict isolation.'

He glanced at Lucy. 'One thing I do want you to be careful about is ensuring that her parents understand the need for taking precautions. Evidently, there was a bit of a problem yesterday when the mother removed her mask. I know it can be hard to make parents understand how vital it is that they stick to the rules, but it is for the child's own benefit.'

She nodded, understanding why he was concerned. A baby this susceptible to infection could succumb even to a common cold. 'Of course, Dr Farrell. I'll have a word with them when they come in to visit,' she assured him.

'Good.' He gave her a brief nod then moved on. They all discarded their protective clothing before continuing the ward round. There were several parents in the unit that morning but Tom made no fuss about them being there. He had a very relaxed attitude to parents, as she remembered from the past. He had always stated that he preferred to have them maybe getting in the way rather than them not bothering to visit, which only upset the child.

She sighed softly as she realised that once again she was letting her mind drift back to the old days. After what she had learned on Saturday surely it was a mistake? Tom most definitely wanted to put it behind him and who could blame him for that?

She forced her mind to go blank at that point, not wanting to start thinking again about what he had told her. Mary Blake, Jonathan's mother, was paying her first visit to the unit that day and Tom stopped to speak to her. A pretty woman in her early twenties, she was standing by the cot stroking Jonathan's hand.

'Hello, Mrs Blake, how nice to see you.' Tom shook

hands with both Mary and David Blake, then glanced at the little boy at their side. 'And who is this, then?'

'This is Daniel,' Mary explained, drawing the child forward. 'He wanted to come and meet his new little brother, didn't you, love?'

Daniel nodded shyly before turning back to stare at the baby in the cot. 'Oh, look, he's smiling at me!' he exclaimed excitedly.

Lucy didn't have the heart to explain that it was probably a touch of wind causing Jonathan to grimace like that! 'He must know that you're his big brother, I expect.'

Daniel nodded importantly. ''Spect so. Mummy said that he'd been sick but that he's getting better now. When can he come home so that I can play with him?'

Lucy ruffled his hair. 'Soon. He just needs to get a little bit stronger.' She looked up and caught Tom's eyes, felt a little colour rush to her cheeks as she saw the expression in them. She wasn't sure what it meant, and before she had time to work it out David Blake claimed his attention by asking about Jonathan's progress.

Tom explained once again how pleased they were with the baby's condition then, once he was sure that Mr and Mrs Blake were quite happy, led the way to baby Rosie's cot. He glanced back and smiled as he saw the family clustered around Jonathan's cot.

'I think that's going to work out all right at the end of the day. They seem to have adapted to the child's handicap remarkably well, wouldn't you say?'

He sighed as he turned his attention to the little girl. 'Let's hope we have a happy ending for this poor little mite.'

'Have the police made any progress yet?' Meredith asked, and once again Lucy noticed the catch in her voice. Baby Rosie seemed to have really touched a chord with Meredith and she found herself wondering why this case more than any of the others seemed to have affected the young doctor.

'I'm afraid not,' Tom replied, sounding disappointed. 'So far nobody has come forward with any information.'

That seemed to put rather a dampener on everyone's spirits. They finished the rest of the round, Tom expressing his pleasure about Liam's progress. The child hadn't suffered any further seizures and the outlook for him was far more positive than it had been.

He drew Lucy aside as they left the child's cot. Rob had been called to the phone and Meredith had disappeared somewhere. 'I thought you'd like to know that Callie has been accepted on the rehabilitation programme,' he informed her. 'She starts next week so it's fingers crossed that she sticks to it.'

'That's brilliant!' she replied sincerely. 'Does she know?'

He nodded. 'Yes. I came in yesterday to check on the Alesi baby and she and Ben were here visiting Liam. I told her then.'

He paused and she had the feeling that there was something else he wanted to say. She looked at him curiously and heard him sigh. 'Look, Lucy, about Saturday night and what I told you about Fiona, I'd be grateful if you kept it to yourself.'

'Of course.' She could barely disguise her hurt that he should have felt it necessary to ask that. Did he really believe that she would betray his confidence?

She gave him a tight smile. 'Don't worry, Tom. I have no intention of spreading gossip about you. I have better ways to spend my time!'

His eyes narrowed as he heard the bite in her voice. 'I'm sure you have. It makes me realise how grateful I should be for all the time you've spared me recently. However, I'm sure you'll be pleased to know that the days of me having to call on you for help are over.'

He shrugged as she glanced at him. 'Adam has been offered a permanent place in the crèche because one of the other children is leaving. And Ruth Jenkins says that her daughter would be happy to babysit for me any time I get called out. Evidently, Jane's at college here in London and looking for a way to earn a bit of extra money to supplement her grant.'

'Good. It seems that things are working out perfectly, doesn't it?'

She turned away, not giving him chance to say anything more. She didn't need to hear it anyway. Tom had made it perfectly clear that he had no more need of her! Was that how he had spent his weekend, making sure that he wouldn't need to involve her in his life ever again?

The thought was so painful that she felt tears burn her eyes and hurriedly left the unit before anyone noticed. She went straight to the ladies' cloakroom and sank down onto a hard plastic chair beside the basins as she struggled to get a grip on herself. It wasn't easy. Working with Tom, and knowing how he felt about her, was just too painful. Maybe she should think about looking for another job?

The toilet flushed and she fixed a smile to her mouth as Meredith appeared from one of the stalls. However, one look at the other woman's ashen face was enough to tell her that something was seriously wrong.

'What is it, Meredith?' she asked, leaping to her feet in concern. 'Here, sit down before you fall down.'

She eased her onto the chair, then hurriedly filled a glass with water and made her take a few sips. 'How long have you felt like this?' she asked worriedly. 'Do you think it's some sort of a bug?'

Meredith shook her head. 'No.' Tears suddenly welled from her eyes. 'I'm pregnant.'

'Oh, dear!' Lucy bent down and gave her a quick hug. 'I suppose it is a case of "oh dear" and not congratulations?'

'I don't know what it is. It wasn't meant to happen. I don't know how it did!' Meredith declared, then blinked when Lucy laughed gently.

'And you a doctor, too? I don't know what they teach

you in med school these days!' She laughed as Meredith gave a grudging smile, although she couldn't help thinking that this certainly explained the other woman's emotional state of late.

'That's better. Now, come on, let's deal with this sensibly. I know you didn't plan it, but it isn't the end of the world,' she said encouragingly.

'I suppose not. It's just that it was such a shock, you see. And…and I've no idea how Rob is going to take the news.' Tears began trickling down Meredith's cheeks again. 'He won't want a baby. He isn't looking for a committed relationship!' she wailed.

'I think you might be surprised. From what I can tell, Rob is very fond of you.' She smiled as Meredith looked at her hopefully. 'He told me all about you not wanting to go out with him any more. He was really cut up about it, too.'

'Was he?' There was a momentary hope in Meredith's eyes before it faded abruptly. 'But you know Rob—he likes a good time and enjoys having a laugh; he isn't looking for responsibility.'

Lucy shrugged. 'Yes, I know all that but I still think that you are misjudging him. I think you should talk to him, tell him about the baby before you decide what you are going to do.'

'I'm going to keep it whatever happens!' Meredith declared, placing a protective hand on her abdomen.

Lucy smiled. 'In that case, then, you are going to *have* to tell Rob. Quite apart from the fact that it isn't going to take him long to put two and two together, it wouldn't be fair not to tell him. This baby is as much his as yours, Meredith. He or she deserves to have both a mother and a father.'

'I know that! Every time I look at little Rosie I keep thinking about how it would be if I didn't tell Rob and…and something happened to me.' She gave a watery smile. 'I suppose I just need to pluck up enough courage,

, but I can't help being scared about how he is going to react.'

'It's always better to tell the truth if you can bring your-self to do so,' Lucy said sadly, wishing that she'd had the courage to follow her own advice five years earlier. She sighed inwardly. But if she had done so then there would be no Adam in the world now and she wouldn't wish for that.

'I suppose you're right.' Meredith sighed as she got up. 'Thanks for listening anyway, Lucy. It has helped to get it off my chest. I've been so worried these past weeks.'

'I understand. But I honestly don't think you have any-thing to fear.' She laughed gently. 'I think Rob is going to make a great father!'

She left Meredith washing her face and went back to the unit. Concentrating on the other woman's problems had taken the edge off her own but at some point soon she would have to make a decision about what to do. If she stayed at Lizzie's then she would have to find a way to work with Tom in some degree of harmony, yet she wasn't sure that was possible. She didn't want to leave because she loved her job and yet the thought of being put through the emotional wringer each day was unbearably painful. Like Meredith, she, too, needed to find the courage to make up her mind.

The next couple of weeks passed uneventfully. Tom was polite and friendly whenever he came into the unit but she was very much aware that he was keeping her at a distance. With Sister Thomas back on duty there was less need for Lucy to come into contact with him, which was a blessing. However, she couldn't help wishing that things might have been different and often found herself indulging in silly little daydreams where Tom suddenly declared his love and they rode off into the sunset together. That certainly wasn't going to happen!

With regard to Meredith and Rob the situation seemed

much the same. She guessed that Meredith was finding it hard to tell Rob about the baby, but it certainly didn't help an already tense situation when she heard via the grapevine that Rob had been taking out Lisa Chan. She wished she could do something but she couldn't break a confidence and interfere. The course of true love never did run smoothly and medical professionals were no better at dealing with it than anyone else, it appeared!

There were a lot of changes on the unit as babies were discharged and others admitted. Jade Jackson went home, as did Jack Williams, both sets of parents being supported by the home care team over the first difficult weeks of adjustment. Both Rosie and Jonathan were making excellent progress and Mary Blake moved into one of the mother and baby rooms a few days prior to taking Jonathan home. Most mothers, even ones who'd had a baby before, found it helped to have time to adapt to the demands of their child before taking him home.

Even Lucia Alesi seemed to be responding well. The good news was that it seemed her immune deficiency disorder was not SCIDS, although more tests would need to be undertaken as she got older. She was still highly susceptible to infection, but the outlook wasn't quite so grim and there was talk of her being flown home to Italy by air ambulance in the not-too-distant future.

Most of the staff were getting themselves geared up for the Valentine's Day dance. Lucy had no intention of going so when Kelly Morris asked her if she would swap shifts and work for her, she readily agreed. Valentine's Day was a time for couples and she most certainly wasn't half of a pair!

That evening Sister Carmichael rang in sick with a heavy cold, which left Lucy in charge. She went and said hello to the rest of the team, then did the rounds.

The evening flew past. There was always so much to do that they were all kept busy. She had a chat with Mary Blake during one of the quieter periods and was struck once again by how well she was coping with Jonathan's disability. Obviously, there might be down periods in the future, but Mary had taken a very positive view and had set about learning all she could about Down's syndrome.

Lucy promised to find her the address of the Down's Syndrome Association then advised her to take a nap before Jonathan woke for his next feed. She went for her break shortly afterwards. It was just before ten and the hospital was quiet, although the faint strains of music from the Valentine's dance came drifting up to the canteen. Several of the staff on duty had gone to join in the fun during their breaks but she didn't bother going down. There was only one person she wanted to be with that night, only one person she wanted to take her in his arms and hold her close, and there was no chance of that happening!

In the end she cut short her break and returned to the unit to find that all hell had broken loose. Jonathan Blake was missing.

CHAPTER TEN

'So, let's run through this one more time, Mrs Blake. When you left the room Jonathan was in his cot? Is that right?'

The police had arrived and Inspector Clarke of the CID was taking Mary Blake back through what had happened leading up to Jonathan's disappearance. There were more police officers taking statements from the staff and helping the hospital's own security men make a search of the whole building. It was like something out of a nightmare and Lucy was having difficulty taking in what was happening.

'That's right. Jonathan was asleep when I went for a shower. I'd just finished when I heard him crying so I hurried up and got out but then he stopped,' Mary explained in a tremulous voice. 'When I went back to the room he wasn't in the cot so I thought one of the staff had heard him crying and taken him back to the unit. But when I went to fetch him they said he wasn't there...'

Her voice broke on a sob as she recalled the moment when she had discovered her baby was missing, and Lucy squeezed her hand. 'It will be all right, Mary. I'm sure Jonathan is going to be fine and that the police will find him.'

'But it's all my fault! If I hadn't left the door open so that I could hear him...' Mary couldn't go on. Lucy bit back a sigh because it was true that this might have been avoided. All the rooms had coded locks, making it impossible for anyone to gain entry unless they knew the correct sequence of numbers to key in. However, it wouldn't help Mary to dwell on that now.

'Nobody would have expected a baby to be taken from

intensive care of all places,' she said soothingly. She looked up as Inspector Clarke asked if he could have a word with her. She left Mary in the care of one of the other nurses and followed him out to the corridor.

'I'm going to need a full description of the child plus some details of his medical history. I believe Jonathan has Down's syndrome?'

'That's right. So he would be easily recognisable,' she confirmed. 'Down's babies have eyes which slope upwards at the outer corners and the backs of their heads are flat rather than rounded. And of course in Jonathan's case he has scars left from his operation.'

'Right. That will help when we need to identify him. Did you say that the consultant in charge is on his way here, by the way?' he asked.

'Dr Farrell? Yes. He shouldn't be long now. He was just trying to arrange a babysitter for his son,' she explained, glancing round as the lift arrived. She felt her heart surge with relief as Tom appeared. 'Here he is now.'

He came straight over to them and the two men shook hands before the police officer quickly repeated his request for details. Tom nodded. 'No problem. I'll get onto it right away. Martyn Lennard, the hospital manager, is on his way here; he said something about you needing a statement for the press?'

'That's right,' the inspector agreed. 'The public are our best allies in a case like this. There's always someone who has noticed something odd, like baby clothes suddenly appearing on a washing line, for instance. The sooner we get the story to the media, the happier I'll be. I'd like to call a press conference for about an hour's time, if that's all right with you?'

'Fine.' Tom sighed heavily. 'It's just so hard to understand why anyone would take a child from here, though, isn't it? It doesn't make sense.'

'It doesn't. But then the one thing cases like this have in common is that the women who take the babies aren't usually behaving rationally,' the inspector replied grimly. 'Anyway, I'll go and see if my men have got anything out of the staff. It's just a shame that it happened tonight when the place was so busy with people coming and going for the dance.'

'Do you think that's how someone managed to slip in?' Lucy asked. 'I mean, the outer doors are kept locked at night and there is always a guard on duty at all the exits. It makes it hard for someone just to wander in off the street.'

'It's a possibility. With all the hustle and bustle that's been going on someone might just have slipped past, although how they got the child out of the building without being noticed, I've no idea.' The inspector shrugged. 'Anyway, I've got a couple of men going through the CCTV tapes. All the exits are covered so let's hope they come up with something soon.'

He hurried away and Tom sighed. 'It's still hard to believe, isn't it? How is Mary coping? Has her husband arrived yet?'

'He's on his way. He had to drop Daniel off at his parents'.' She followed him into the office and sank down onto a chair, feeling suddenly drained now that reaction was starting to set in. Having a baby go missing was every member of staff's worst nightmare. 'Who did you manage to get to babysit for Adam, by the way?'

'Ruth Jenkins. I rang to ask her daughter if she would come round but Ruth volunteered as soon as she discovered what had happened.' He went to the window and stared out across the park, his face set into a frown of concern. It was pitch-black outside and Lucy shivered as she thought about little Jonathan being out there with a stranger.

'I hope whoever has taken him realises just how vulnerable he is,' she said in a shaky voice. 'I know he's recovered from his operations but he still needs to be kept warm and it must be bitter out there tonight.'

'I'm sure he'll be fine, Lucy,' Tom said softly, turning

to look at her. 'Most babies who are abducted are well cared for. You know that.'

'I know, but it doesn't help!' She stood up and began pacing the room. 'I keep going over and over what went on tonight, wondering if it could have been avoided if I'd done things differently. I mean, if I hadn't gone for my break when I did and maybe spent more time making sure that Mary understood how important it was to always lock her door…'

'Hey, come on! It isn't your fault. Nobody could have foretold this was going to happen, so you mustn't go blaming yourself.' Tom crossed the room and took hold of her by the shoulders. 'It isn't your fault, Lucy!'

'Isn't it? What if the police don't find Jonathan? Or if something happens to him?' She shuddered as her mind ran riot. He sighed as he drew her into his arms and held her tightly.

'It won't. You have to hang onto that thought. Jonathan will be fine. I promise you.' He held her close until the spasm passed, yet even then he didn't immediately let her go as she'd expected him to. She took a small breath as the warmth of his body began to seep into her own and warm away the chill which had invaded it. When Tom held her like this it was easy to believe that things would turn out all right, but why should that be a surprise? The safest place in the world had always been right here, in Tom's arms, and how she wished that she could stay here for ever!

She must have made some small sound as the thought registered because he bent to look at her. 'Are you OK?' he asked with such concern that tears sprang to her eyes. He grimaced as he saw them, his arms tightening as he drew her even closer.

'Shh, don't upset yourself. It will be all right, you'll see. The police will find Jonathan and he'll be back here in no time at all,' he assured her in a velvety soft voice which instantly dried her tears as it sent a wave of heat rippling through her body.

'I…I suppose you're right,' she stammered. Suddenly the feel of his strong body so close to hers was less comforting than stimulating. She was achingly conscious of how her breasts were beginning to throb as they were crushed against the hard wall of his chest.

She took a quick breath but it did more harm than good as she felt her nipples tauten as they brushed against his chest. Could Tom feel how her body was responding to his nearness? she wondered giddily, and couldn't stop herself from looking up.

Their eyes met and held in a look which made her heart race because suddenly she knew that she wasn't the only one affected by the intimacy of the moment. She could see the same awareness in Tom's eyes.

He gave a rough little murmur as his hand lifted to cup her cheek. 'Lucy, I—'

He got no further as there was a sudden knock on the door at that moment. He let her go and went to answer it while she struggled to control the crazy beating of her heart. It wasn't easy because what she had seen in Tom's eyes made her blood race just to recall it. He had looked at her with such *hunger* just now that it both shocked and thrilled her. It was only when she saw the urgency on Inspector Clarke's face as he came into the room that she managed to pull herself together.

'Can you come, both of you? One of the security staff can hear a baby crying in the underground car park. They're searching all the cars at the moment,' he explained tersely. 'They also got this off one of the CCTV monitors covering the car park entrance. It's the only car which has come in or out in the past hour.'

He handed Tom a fuzzy photograph which had been taken from the video tape. Lucy peered over his shoulder and gasped as she recognised the driver. 'That's Emma Foster!'

'You know her?' the policeman demanded, leading the way to the lifts at a brisk pace. 'So is she staff or what?'

'No. Her baby was in here a few weeks ago. Unfortunately, the child died,' Tom explained succinctly as they made their way down to the car park. 'Emma took it especially hard and we were extremely concerned about her, so much so that we got in touch with her GP to advise him of the situation.'

'Seems to fit,' Inspector Clarke agreed as the lift stopped. 'Most cases like this we find the woman has lost a baby of her own.' He hurried over to where his officers were talking to one of the hospital's own security staff and came back a few moments later.

'Right, they've located the car on the next level up but they didn't want to do anything to scare the woman in case she tried to drive off. Obviously, the last thing we want is anyone getting hurt. We need someone to talk to her, preferably someone she knows.'

'I'll do it,' Lucy offered immediately. 'Emma knows me.'

'Good.' Inspector Clarke cautiously led the way up the ramp and pointed to a small Ford parked all askew a few yards away. Even though its doors were closed, they could hear the baby crying. 'Right, we won't do anything until we get your say-so, but be very careful. My guess is that she'll be in a highly emotional state, wouldn't you agree, Doc?'

'Most certainly. She is likely to behave very irrationally so don't do anything to panic her, Lucy. Just try talking to her and see if you can persuade her to give Jonathan to you. But if you're at all worried then I want you to promise that you'll leave the police to handle things. Don't put yourself at risk,' Tom advised her, outwardly calm, but she wasn't deaf to the concern in his voice.

'I'll be fine,' she assured him softly. He gave her shoulder a quick squeeze and she felt her breath catch as she saw the expression in his eyes. Maybe it was the muted lighting, but she could almost believe that he really felt something for her when he looked at her like that!

She pushed that thought to the back of her mind as she made her way towards the car. She needed to focus all her attention on dealing with this delicate situation so couldn't allow her mind to wander. But just knowing that Tom was there was a comfort.

Emma Foster was sitting in the driving seat, holding Jonathan on her knee. She didn't appear to have noticed Lucy approaching so she tapped on the window.

'Emma, it's me, Lucy,' she said softly, seeing the alarm which immediately contorted the woman's face.

'Go away!' Emma shouted, fumbling with the ignition, and Lucy's heart turned over. Somehow she had to stop Emma from driving off.

'Look, Emma, I only want to talk to you,' she declared, crouching down so that she could peer through the car window. 'You know you don't have to be scared of me, don't you?'

A look of indecision crossed Emma's face. 'What do you want to talk about?'

'There are things you need to know about Jonathan,' she said off the top of her head.

'Well…' Emma hesitated. It was obvious that she was undecided what to do, so Lucy took advantage of the opportunity afforded her.

'Look, can I just get into the car for a moment?' She rubbed her hands up and down her arms. 'It's really cold out here and I haven't got a coat with me.'

'I suppose so. But you have to promise that you won't try to take him away from me,' Emma declared. 'Nobody is going to take my baby away ever again!'

'I promise, Emma. And you know you can trust me.' Lucy's heart ached at the pain she heard in the other woman's voice. It was impossible to imagine what poor Emma was going through right then.

Emma hesitated a moment longer, then suddenly reached over and unlocked the passenger door. Lucy hurried round the vehicle and got in. She lowered the window so that she would be able to speak to the police if need be, then gave Emma a reassuring smile, noticing immediately how unkempt she looked. Her brown hair was badly in need of washing and her clothes looked as though she had slept in them. She felt suddenly angry that Emma's husband had allowed her to get in this state. Surely he must have realised that she needed help?

'Why did you take Jonathan out of his cot?' she asked quietly, wondering if it would help if she found out what had motivated Emma to take the baby that night.

'Because he was crying, of course.' Emma looked at her in surprise. 'You shouldn't leave a baby crying like that. It isn't right. All he wanted was to be picked up and cuddled.'

'So you decided to look after him, did you? Well, that was kind of you, Emma, but maybe we should take him back inside now.' She smiled as Jonathan let out an angry wail. 'I think he's hungry, from the sound of it.'

'No!' Emma clutched the baby to her. 'I'm not taking him back. He belongs to me now and I'm going to take care of him.'

'You know that isn't true, Emma,' she said firmly. 'Jonathan has a mother and a father, even a little brother, who all love him very much. His mother is upstairs crying her heart out because she's so worried about him.'

'But I'll look after him. You can tell her that, Lucy. You know that I'll love him, don't you?'

Lucy swallowed as she heard the despair in Emma's voice. 'Yes, I know that you would never harm Jonathan. But you can't keep him. His parents need him.'

'But I need him!' Tears began to stream down Emma's face. 'Peter said that he's leaving me. He said that he wants a divorce, but he'll change his mind when he sees the baby. He'll have to stay then, won't he? He always wanted a son, you see. And we'll be so happy then, the three of us.'

Lucy bit back a sigh. Why on earth hadn't Peter Foster had the sense to realise what he was doing? However, there was no time to dwell on it as Emma started fumbling with the ignition once more.

'But Jonathan isn't your baby, Emma,' she said quickly to distract her. She caught a movement out of the corner of her eye and knew that the police were closing in. She didn't dare think what would happen if Emma saw them.

She forced herself to speak calmly even though her heart was racing. 'I know how much you must miss Abigail, but it isn't right to make Jonathan's mother go through all that pain, is it?'

'But she can have another baby! You just said that she already has a little boy. All I want is a baby of my own to love...' Emma broke off on a sob.

'I know and I understand how you feel.' She took a deep breath because suddenly she knew that the best way to get through to Emma was to be truthful.

'Many times I've held a baby in my arms and wished that it could be mine. I know how it feels to long for a child to love and take care of, you see.' She smiled wistfully as Emma looked up. It was obvious that she had gained her attention so she carried on, unaware of the pain which touched her voice.

'I can't have children, you see. I had cancer when I was younger and the treatment I received means that I can never have a baby of my own. The doctors explained it all to me at the time but there wasn't anything they could do. If I hadn't agreed to have the treatment then I would have died.

'So, I do understand how you feel, Emma. I know how empty you must feel and how you ache to hold your own baby in your arms because that's how I feel. I know how much you must miss Abigail, but at least you still have the memory of her in your heart, where it matters most. And one day there might be another baby to love, another new life to cherish and take care of, but not this one. Jonathan doesn't belong to you and you must be brave enough to give him back to his mother.'

She held her breath as she finished speaking, wondering

if she had managed to get through to Emma. She could have wept for joy when the woman slowly held Jonathan towards her. Lucy opened the door as the police came rushing over but it was Tom's arm which looped around her waist to support her as she stepped from the car.

'Are you OK?'

She looked up into his face and saw the pain which darkened his eyes. Had he heard what she had said? Was he wondering why she had kept it a secret from him? Her heart turned over at the thought because she wasn't sure what she would tell him if he demanded an explanation.

'I'm fine,' she assured him, striving to sound normal. 'But I could do with a cup of tea!'

He laughed as she'd intended him to. However, there was a note in his voice which warned her that, although he might be willing to let things lie for now, it certainly wasn't the end of the matter. 'Let's just get this young man back upstairs, then I'll treat you to a nice hot cuppa to celebrate a job well done!'

He steered her towards the lift but she hung back as she saw two police officers escorting Emma to their car. 'Where are they taking her?' she asked worriedly. 'Surely they realise that she is ill and aren't going to charge her?'

'They'll have to take her to the station to get a statement, but she will be moved to a hospital as soon as they've interviewed her, I imagine.' Tom sighed. 'I can't help feeling that we should have done something more for her.'

'We did all we could. She told me that her husband had left her. I think it was that which finally tipped her over the edge,' Lucy explained sadly.

Tom gripped her shoulder and there was a note of real anguish in his voice. 'I know. We could hear what was being said, Lucy. It…it was very moving.'

She knew he wasn't referring just to what Emma had said but, thankfully, he didn't say anything more as he escorted her back up to the department. Mary and David Blake were overjoyed to have Jonathan back. Tom let them hold him while he briefly explained what had happened, then whisked the baby away to check him over. News of the incident must have spread to the dance floor because several members of staff arrived to find out what had been going on.

Lucy went through it all again, modestly downplaying her part in bringing events to their happy conclusion. She had just finished when Martyn Lennard appeared, wanting a full account as well. It was obvious that he intended to grill her there and then, only just at that moment Tom arrived back and stepped in.

'Look, Martyn, I suggest we leave this till a later date. Lucy has been through enough tonight and she needs to go home and rest.' He held his hand up when she went to protest that she was all right. 'No, it was nerve-racking just watching what was happening, let alone being involved as you were. I've arranged cover for you.'

'Well, I suppose you're right,' Martyn conceded. He patted her on the shoulder. 'Well done, Lucy. If it weren't for you, things might not have turned out nearly so well. Do what Tom says and get yourself off home now. You're off tomorrow, I believe, so we'll have a chat when you're back at work.'

'Well, if you're sure...' she said hesitantly, suddenly realising just how exhausted she felt.

'I am,' Martyn assured her. She left him talking to Tom as she went to fetch her coat, then took the lift to the ground floor. It was just gone midnight and there was a crowd of revellers leaving the dance. She was soon caught up as they crowded around her to hear what had happened. She went through the story one more time, groaning as more people arrived and demanded to know what had gone on. At this rate she would never get away!

'OK, folks, that's it for tonight. Let's give Lucy a break, eh? I'm sure we'll be able to read the full story about our very own heroine's exploits in the morning papers.'

Rob Turner materialised at her side to rescue her. There

was a bit of good-natured grumbling, but gradually the crowd dispersed. He turned to her, frowning in concern as he saw how pale she looked.

'Are you all right, Lucy?'

'Yes,' she began, then grimaced. In all honesty she felt far from all right. In fact, she was beginning to feel both physically and emotionally drained as reaction set in. 'Not really.'

'Then let's get you home. I've a taxi waiting outside so I'll drop you off.' Rob took her arm and led her swiftly out to where the taxi was waiting. He helped her inside then gave the driver her address and got in beside her.

Lucy sank back into the seat, grateful to leave it to him to take charge. The cab swung round to head back out to the street and drew level with the main doors of the hospital once more. She felt her heart leap as she saw Tom standing there. For a moment their eyes met and she felt pain lance through her as she saw the anguish on his face before the taxi drove on.

'Do you want me to ask the driver to stop?' Rob offered, looking back at the lone figure silhouetted against the brightly lit foyer.

She shook her head, unaware that tears were sliding silently down her face. 'No. I…I just want to go home,' she whispered.

Rob didn't question her any more but she wasn't blind to the concern on his face. She closed her eyes, not wanting to have to explain what was wrong. She couldn't have done that, not then. But at some point soon she would have to explain to Tom what he had overheard in the car park that night. It was an explanation which was probably long overdue, but that didn't mean it was going to be easy to tell him the truth after all this time. She couldn't bear to imagine how he would react when he discovered she had lied to him…

It was a little after eight the next morning when there was a knock on the front door. Lucy hadn't slept, her mind too full of everything that had happened to allow her to rest. She had got up before the first grey light of dawn had touched the sky and sat in the lounge while she tried to think what she was going to tell Tom. But as she opened the door and found him outside she still had no real idea how to go about it.

'Hello, Lucy. How are you?'

There were dark circles under his eyes which told their own tale and her heart contracted on a spasm of pain as she saw them. Had Tom spent the night thinking about what he had overheard and trying to make sense of it?

Deep down, she knew that was so and it didn't help. Obviously, it had been playing on his mind as much as it had on hers, but she still couldn't think of an easy way round the situation other than to tell him the truth. Yet she quailed at the thought of doing that because of what else she would have to reveal.

Would it serve any purpose now to let Tom know that the only reason she had lied to him had been because she had loved him so much? She doubted it!

She took a quick breath as she realised he was waiting for her to answer. 'I'm fine. I…I suppose you'd better come in. We can't talk on the step.'

He came inside, then stopped and looked around, a frown darkening his brow as he took note of the drawn curtains. Although she had been up for some time she hadn't bothered drawing them back and the room looked shadowy in the grey morning light filtering through the fabric. His mouth thinned as he turned to glance at the bedroom door before he let his eyes travel deliberately over the pale blue robe she was wearing over her nightdress.

'Obviously, it was a mistake to turn up unannounced like this,' he stated flatly. 'I should have phoned first. I apologise. It certainly wasn't my intention to make things awkward for you.'

'Awkward?' she repeated blankly, wondering what on earth he meant.

'Yes, awkward!' He swore impatiently, running a hand through his hair to push the heavy strands back from his forehead. 'Surely I don't need to spell it out for you, Lucy? I know that Rob brought you home last night. I should have thought about that before I came here and I apologise. However, there are things we need to discuss, so maybe you could meet me later if it isn't convenient right now. Give me a call when you're free.'

'Just a second.' She stopped him as he swung round to leave, her temper rising to dizzying heights as she realised what he had meant. 'Before you go any further I think we need to clear something up: *yes*, Rob did bring me home last night but, *no*, he didn't stay.' She strode to the bedroom and flung the door open. 'So you aren't making things *awkward* at all, Tom!'

'But I thought…' He stopped abruptly, his eyes going to the empty bed before he gave a weary sigh which tugged at her heartstrings despite how angry she felt about the assumption he had made. 'I guess it's obvious what I thought and I'm sorry, Lucy. I seem to make rather a habit of adding things up and coming up with the wrong answers, don't I?'

'In this case, yes,' she agreed. She went to the window and drew back the curtains, then turned to him again. 'There is nothing going on between Rob and me, Tom. I think I told you that once before.'

'I know you did. I'm sorry. I don't know what's the matter with me lately. I feel as though I don't know whether I'm on my head or my heels most of the time.'

She smiled sadly, her temper disappearing almost as fast as it had come because she understood only too well what he meant. 'I know how you feel.'

'Do you, Lucy?'

There was a sudden urgency in his voice, an expression in his eyes which made her heart race as she saw it. She took a quick breath but it did nothing to dispel the tension which beset her all of a sudden. What did Tom want her to say? she wondered shakily. Did he want her to admit that it was ever since *he* had come back into her life that she'd had such difficulty keeping things on an even keel?

It seemed the only logical explanation and yet she shied away from admitting it because she was scared of how vulnerable it might make her. She gave a small shrug instead. 'Yes, of course. It's been so hectic lately that it's little wonder everything seems to be in constant turmoil.'

'Especially last night,' he agreed, but there was a note in his voice which told her that he knew she was trying to gloss over the real issue.

'Have you heard how Emma Foster is?' she asked quickly, latching onto the first thing she could think of.

'I spoke to Inspector Clarke before I left home. Emma has been transferred to a psychiatric unit for assessment. They will decide whether or not to press charges once they have a report, but the inspector doesn't think it likely.' Tom sighed heavily. 'Evidently, Peter Foster not only told her that he wanted a divorce, but that he has a girlfriend who is three months pregnant. I think *that* was what tipped Emma over the edge.'

'Oh, the poor thing!' Lucy sank down on a chair, her brown eyes full of compassion at the thought of what Emma had been going through. 'No wonder she went off the rails like that.'

'Exactly.' Tom sat down as well. 'All we can do now is to make sure that she gets the help she needs, but it's thanks to you, Lucy, that things turned out as well as they did. If you hadn't managed to persuade her to hand Jonathan over, then heaven alone knows what might have happened.'

She wasn't deaf to the rough grate of his voice and she knew without a shadow of doubt that he was thinking about what he had overheard the previous night. When he suddenly looked up there was a world of sadness in his eyes.

'Why didn't you tell me that you couldn't have children, Lucy? I've spent the night going over and over it, but I still don't understand why you kept it a secret from me.'

She had to swallow the lump in her throat as she heard the anguish in his voice. That Tom was hurting was beyond question and suddenly she knew that, no matter what happened or what repercussions it might have, she had to tell him the truth. If nothing else she owed him that!

'Be…because I knew how you would react,' she said in a husky little whisper.

'How I would react?' he repeated before his face suddenly contorted with pain. 'Surely you didn't think that I would be like Peter Foster, that I wouldn't want you if I found out that you couldn't give me a child?' he demanded harshly.

'No! Of course not!' She jumped to her feet, unable to sit there calmly while he made such wildly inaccurate assumptions. 'I never imagined that you would react like that, Tom, and that's the truth!'

'Then I don't understand!' He stood up as well, big and imposing as he towered over her. 'For pity's sake, Lucy, you can't leave it at that. You have to explain!'

There was no denying the urgency in his voice and she smiled sadly. 'Because I knew that if I told you that I couldn't give you a child you would claim it didn't matter.' She took a small breath, then looked him straight in the eyes so that he would see that she was telling the truth.

'I knew how much you wanted a family, Tom, and I couldn't let that happen. I couldn't deny you something you wanted so much, you see.'

'The only thing I wanted was you!' He reached out and gripped hold of her by the shoulders, His hands bit into her flesh but she knew that he wasn't aware of what he was doing at that moment. 'I was crazy about you, Lucy! If I wanted a child so much it was because it would be our child, the one you and I created together. If you'd told me the truth then it wouldn't have changed how I felt about you!'

'How can you be sure? Oh, it's easy to say that now, but perhaps there would have come a time when you'd have felt differently. Maybe at some point you might even have come to…to hate me for ruining all your hopes and dreams.'

She was unaware that tears were streaming down her face as she looked at him with all the anguish she had felt five years before clear to see on her face. 'I couldn't bear the thought of that ever happening, Tom, which is why I decided that I had to end our relationship. There wasn't anything else I could do.'

He went absolutely still. She could feel the tension emanating from him at that moment and her head swirled as she was caught up in the sheer force of emotion. There was a rawness to his voice when he spoke, an edge which made her breath catch as she heard it. That he was struggling to hold himself in check was obvious and her heart ran wild as she wondered what might happen next.

'What about the guy you left me for? I thought you had decided that we didn't have a future because you had fallen in love with someone else?'

'There…there wasn't anyone else. I made that up. I…I knew that I had to find a way to convince you that it was over, Tom. And that was the best way I could think of,' she admitted in a husky little whisper.

He took a deep breath, then closed his eyes almost as though he couldn't bear to look at her at that moment. 'So everything you told me was a lie? There was no one else and you didn't leave Derbyshire to be with him?' His eyes opened to bore straight into hers and she lowered her head, unable to stand there and face him now that he knew what she had done. She couldn't bear to imagine what he must think about her now!

'Yes. It…it was all lies, Tom,' she admitted in a choked voice.

He slid his hand beneath her chin and forced her to look at him. 'Why did you do it, Lucy? Oh, I know what you just said, that you didn't want to deny me the family I longed for and couldn't bear the thought that I might come to hate you at some point, but surely it must have been a difficult decision for you to make?' He shrugged but there was an intentness to the look he gave her. 'I mean, you left your home and family, a job you loved; it was a huge step to take. You could simply have told me that you no longer wanted to go out with me and left it at that.'

She shook her head. 'No, I couldn't have done that. I…I had to get away…'

She broke off, suddenly realising what she had said. She heard Tom take a deep breath but his voice sounded hoarse when he spoke, as though there weren't enough air in the world to let him ask the question easily.

'Why? Why was it so important that you put all that distance between us?'

'I…' She stopped again, unable to answer the simple question because she was afraid.

'Tell me, sweetheart. Please.' The tender entreaty in his voice brought a lump to her throat and she looked at him through a mist of tears. Maybe it would be a mistake to make this final admission, but suddenly she couldn't keep it to herself any longer.

'Because I knew that if I stayed in Derbyshire we would be bound to come into contact and I couldn't bear that, Tom. I couldn't bear to see you each day and keep on pretending about how I felt,' she whispered huskily.

'And how did you feel?' he asked softly. He tilted her face that little bit more, his eyes tender as he wiped away her tears with his thumbs. 'Tell me the truth, Lucy…all of it.'

The husky plea was just too hard to resist so that suddenly she didn't have the strength to hold out a moment longer. 'I loved you, Tom. That's why I couldn't bear to be around you all the time. I knew that if I stayed I would have to tell you the truth about myself and I couldn't take that risk. I…I loved you too much to spoil your life!'

'Oh, my darling, you could never have done that!' He brushed her mouth with the lightest, gentlest of kisses yet one which stirred her unbearably as she felt the promise it held. When he drew back to look at her she felt her pulse leap as she saw the expression in his eyes.

'There is just one more thing we need to clear up, darling.' He smiled at her, his grey eyes tender and adoring. 'You just said that you loved me. But is that past tense only?'

She closed her eyes, knowing there was no hope that she would be able to behave sensibly if she looked into his beloved face...

But did she want to be *sensible*? a small voice whispered seductively. Surely she had done the sensible thing five years before and look where it had got her. Maybe it was time to listen to her heart, not her head...

'Love...as in the present tense, Tom,' she said quickly before her courage deserted her. She opened her eyes and smiled at him, hearing the swift indrawn breath he took. Suddenly she knew that everything was going to be all right. 'I did love you, I do love you, I shall love you. No matter which way you conjugate the verb it still sounds...'

'Perfect!' he finished for her, lowering his head to take her mouth in a kiss of such hunger, such passion, that her blood seemed to turn to molten lava inside her veins.

Lucy uttered a soft little moan, then simply gave herself up to the sheer magic of his kiss. Reaching up, she looped her arms around his neck and drew his head down so that she could return the kiss with an equal fervour. They were both breathless when Tom finally drew back several delicious minutes later.

'I love you, my darling Lucy. I have always loved you and I always shall.'

'But...but are you sure?' she asked tremulously, then blushed when he laughed sexily.

'Very sure. I suppose I should spend the next hour or so explaining it all to you, but I can think of a far better way to convince you—if you are interested, of course?'

She laughed wickedly as she wriggled out of his arms.

'I think I should warn you that I can be very difficult to convince, Dr Farrell.'

He captured her easily, sweeping her up into his arms and grinning as he heard her gasp of surprise. 'That's what I was hoping!'

CHAPTER ELEVEN

THEY made love slowly, the pale rays of light filtering through the curtained window adding a dream-like magic to the scene. Odd, but, even though both of them were so hungry for the other, there seemed no reason to rush. Each kiss was to be savoured, each caress to be enjoyed. It had been so long since she had lain in Tom's arms and let him love her that there was a newness about it which added an extra intensity to the familiar touch of his hands stroking her skin, the remembered weight of his strong body as it settled over hers. When they joined together in the final act of loving, Lucy knew that she would remember this moment for ever. She had come home at last to the one place where she had longed to be…in Tom's arms.

They must have dozed for a while because when she awoke pale winter sunlight was pouring through the window. She sat up, propping herself against the pillows and smiling as Tom suddenly appeared carrying a tray holding two mugs of coffee. He set it down on the bedside table, then bent to kiss her with a hunger which seemed undiminished by the time they had spent making love such a short while before.

Lucy gave a soft little murmur of delight as she reached up to twine her fingers in the cool thick hair at the back of his head and he groaned deeply. Easing his mouth away from hers, he managed to mutter, 'You don't make it easy, sweetheart.'

'Mmm?' She let her lips trail down his cheek to the strong line of his jaw, tracing the angular line with butterfly-soft kisses and smiling as she heard the groan he gave. 'Don't make what easy?'

'To resist you long enough so that we can get some details sorted out,' he muttered thickly.

'What details...?' she began, then gasped as he suddenly sank down onto the bed and rolled her over so that she was lying on top of him.

He kissed her mouth, then her eyelids and the tip of her nose, smiling smugly as he felt her go pliant in his arms. 'Oh, all sorts of things, like where we are going to live after we are married, for starters. I suppose my flat would be better than yours because it's bigger, but—'

'Hold it right there!' She drew back and glared at him, the effect somewhat spoiled by their position. It was hard to appear stern when she was lying on top of him, her soft breasts crushed against the hardness of his chest!

She took a quick breath, trying to focus on what he had said, but it wasn't the easiest thing she'd ever had to do. 'Don't you think you are rather jumping the gun? I don't recall you asking me to marry you, for starters!'

'Didn't I?' He appeared not the least bit abashed as he lifted his head and buzzed her mouth with another kiss, taking his time so that she was trembling when he finally drew back.

'I...er... No!' she managed, but it was an effort. She tried to free herself, deeming it wiser to put a little space between them while they talked about something so important, but he refused to let her go. His eyes were very dark as he looked at her.

'Then it's an oversight I intend to correct this very minute. I love you, Lucy Benson. I made the mistake of letting you go five years ago and I don't intend to make the same mistake now.'

'Are you sure, Tom? I mean, everything has happened so quickly...' She took a deep breath, wanting with all her heart to believe what he was saying, and yet she was afraid that he might regret it once the heat of the moment had passed.

'Maybe it would be best if you took some time to think about it first,' she suggested softly and saw him frown.

'What is there to think about?' he demanded. He framed her face between his hands. 'I love you, Lucy. I don't want to spend the rest of my life regretting the fact that I didn't make it clear how I felt—as I've regretted it so many times these past five years.'

'What do you mean?' she asked, a sudden frown drawing her silky brows together.

'That if I'd told you how much I loved you five years ago then maybe you would have realised that we could have worked things out?' He smoothed the tiny furrows away with a gentle finger but it was impossible not to see the sadness in his eyes when he looked at her.

She shook her head, hating to see him blaming himself for something he couldn't have changed. 'No, it wouldn't have made any difference, Tom. I...I knew how you felt about me, you see. I knew that you were in love with me and that was what made it so hard to do what I thought was right. The thought that I was hurting you was almost unbearably painful, but I did what I had to because I honestly believed that it was the only way to ensure you would get what you wanted so much.'

'A child?' He sighed heavily. 'At one point, a couple of weeks back, I wondered if that had been the reason you had ended our relationship, funnily enough.'

'What do you mean?'

'Oh, it was just something you said, about me wanting a family so much; I did wonder if I had scared you off because you weren't ready to have children,' he admitted softly.

'Oh, Tom!' Tears misted her eyes and he groaned as he quickly kissed them away.

'Don't, sweetheart! I can't bear to see you crying. I just wish that I'd known...' There was a world of regret in his deep voice and she smiled through her grief.

'I took care that you didn't find out, so you mustn't

blame yourself. All I ever wanted was for you to be happy, Tom, and have what you wanted. In a way it worked because you met Fiona and had Adam.'

'Yes. He was the one good thing to come out of our marriage,' he admitted quietly. 'When things were at their worst between Fiona and me I tried to keep that in sight.'

'When you told me what you had gone through I didn't know what to say,' she confessed sadly. 'I'd always hoped that you would meet someone else, even though the thought of you with another woman hurt so much. But when you admitted that your marriage had been a sham I felt so guilty. I kept wondering if…if you hated me because I was the cause of all your unhappiness.'

'No!' He groaned deeply. 'Is that why you went rushing off that night after I'd told you? I thought I'd scared you off and that you were afraid I might be expecting something from you by pouring out my heart like that.'

His laughter was rueful all of a sudden. 'I got it into my head that you had decided that you didn't want to get involved any further. And who could blame you? Why would you choose to get caught up with a widower with a small son and a lot of debts when you had other options?'

'What other options…? You mean Rob?' She glared at him. 'For the hundredth time, Rob was never part of the equation. In case you haven't noticed, he is crazy about Meredith!'

'Meredith? But I thought…' He broke off and grimaced. 'So that explains the atmosphere of late?'

'Uh-huh. Starting to get the picture now, Dr Farrell?' She sighed theatrically. 'Honestly, for a man who is usually so perceptive you seem to have had your head in the sand recently. You must be the only one in the entire hospital who believes that Rob and I are an item!'

He frowned. 'What do you mean?'

She brushed his mouth with a kiss, drawing back before he had time to respond as a small punishment for his blindness, although it was questionable who was being punished when she felt her own hunger surge to life. 'Oh, only that everyone in the place thinks that you and I have something going. The gossip-mongers have had a field-day recently!'

'Have they, indeed?' He grinned wickedly as he suddenly rolled her over, trapping her between the mattress and his body. 'In that case, nobody will be shocked when they hear that we are getting married, will they?'

'Oh, no, you don't get out of it that easily!' She shook her head, smiling as she saw his confusion. 'I want a proper proposal, Tom Farrell. I've waited long enough for it!'

'Five...very...long...years.' He punctuated each word with a kiss, laughing as he saw the dreamy expression in her eyes. His face sobered all of a sudden, his eyes velvety dark as they held hers. 'And they were long years, Lucy, long and empty and lonely. Finding you again seems like a miracle because I never dreamt that it could happen.'

'It feels like that to me, too, Tom.' She cupped his face, 'I love you, my darling. I love you so much that I don't know how to make you believe how much. And I can't think of anything I want more than to spend my life with you, so long as you're sure it's what you want.'

'It is...more than anything.' He kissed her gently. 'Will you marry me, Lucy? I know I haven't got a lot to offer, but everything I have is yours, including Adam.'

She could barely see through the veil of tears. 'I wanted so much to have your child, Tom,' she whispered brokenly.

He kissed her hard and fiercely. 'And now you shall! Adam will be your son as well as mine, my love.'

'Oh, Tom!' She returned his kiss, letting her lips give him the answer he wanted. They were both trembling when they drew apart. Tom nestled her head into the crook of his shoulder, his hand gentle as he tilted her face so that he could bestow a tender kiss on her lips.

'I'm so happy, Lucy. Not just for myself, either. Adam deserves to have someone like you in his life because he has missed so much.'

'Thank you. I can't tell you how wonderful it is to hear

you say that, especially when I sensed that you were determined to keep me at a distance in the beginning,' she whispered.

He grimaced. 'Was it that obvious?' He sighed when she nodded. 'I suppose it was. The trouble was that I was scared to let you back into my life.'

'In case I hurt you again?' She propped herself up on her elbow, her brown eyes filled with regret. 'I'm so sorry, Tom.'

'It doesn't matter now. I understand why you did what you thought was right.' He ran a gentle finger down her cheek, smiling as he felt her shiver. 'I love you, Lucy Benson; how long is it since I told you that?'

She smiled at him, her eyes adoring. 'Oh, at least two minutes, which is far too long, I'd say!' She bent forward and kissed him, then settled back in the crook of his arm again. 'I have to confess that I've felt in a complete turmoil these past few weeks. I kept getting these mixed signals from you!'

He laughed wryly. 'I don't doubt it! It was one thing *deciding* to keep you at arm's length, but quite another to actually do it! Every time I saw you it was that bit more difficult, especially when I watched you with Adam. I tried telling myself that it was natural that I should still feel something for you, but I think I knew from the beginning that it was more than just shared memories which drew us together.'

He sighed ruefully, his grey eyes full of amusement. 'I'm nothing if not stubborn, so I managed to hold out until that afternoon we spent in the park and then I realised how stupid it was. I wanted you back in my life, Lucy. It was as simple as that. I made up my mind that I would tell you that and try to sort things out after I got back from the hospital that evening.'

'Only things didn't quite go to plan and you ended up telling me about your marriage to Fiona instead,' she finished quietly.

'Yes.' He sighed as he drew her closer. 'After that, things seemed to go from bad to worse. I convinced myself that it was a good job that I hadn't said anything as you obviously weren't interested.'

'How wrong could you have been?' She kissed him quickly then rolled over and stood up. Crossing the room, she picked up her robe from where it had been abandoned on the floor a short time before and quickly pulled it on.

Tom sat up, a frown darkening his brow as he looked at her in bewilderment. 'What's going on?'

'Well, we can't stay here all day,' she said briskly, walking to the wardrobe to hunt through the rails. 'We have things to do.'

'What things?' he demanded, sounding less than pleased by the announcement.

She hid her grin as she took a clean pair of jeans off a hanger. 'Oh, all sorts of things. Right, do you want to shower first or shall I?'

He was out of the bed before she had barely finished the sentence, his arms fastening tightly around her as he swung her up into the air. 'We shall both shower…together,' he replied in a tone which brought an immediate blush to her cheeks.

He laughed wickedly as he saw it, bending to kiss her with a thoroughness which made it hard for her to think straight as he continued. 'But only after you tell me what is so urgent that it needs us to get up and dressed this very minute.'

'Making arrangements for our wedding. After all, we've waited five years, Tom, so I can't see any point in waiting any longer, can you?' She smiled into his face, seeing the joy which lit his eyes. 'How does the end of the month sound to you—assuming we can get everything arranged in time, of course?'

'Oh, Lucy…!' He kissed her hard and hungrily, then suddenly set her back down on her feet. Catching hold of her hand, he led her towards the bathroom at a rate of knots, grinning as she gave a little murmur of protest. 'Come on, sweetheart, you said it yourself…we have a lot of time to make up for, so let's not waste another second. You and I have a wedding to arrange!'

Lucy smiled at the excitement she could hear in his voice. She could feel it, too, building inside her. This was the first day of the rest of her life and it was going to be marvellous!

'The end of the month? This month, as in two weeks' time, you mean…?' Megan broke off and swallowed. 'I don't know what to say, quite frankly!'

'Well, that must be a first!' Lucy laughed at her friend's astonishment although it was understandable, really. If anyone had told her twenty-four hours earlier that she would be getting married at the end of February she would have laughed out loud. Yet events had moved with an almost dizzying speed as she and Tom had set about making the arrangements. Now she sat Megan down with a cup of tea as she ran through them once more as much for her own benefit as her friend's. It really *was* hard to take it all in!

'We're having the actual ceremony here in the hospital's chapel. Tom and I thought it would be easier for anyone who might be working that day. My sister is going to be matron of honour and my niece will be a bridesmaid, plus little Adam is going to be a page-boy.' She grinned. 'You won't believe this, but I even found the most perfect dress in a little boutique off Regent Street. It fits like a dream!'

'And you expect me to believe that you got this all sorted out in a single day?' Megan shook her head decisively. 'No way, Lucy Benson! It takes months of blood and sweat, not to mention tears, to plan a wedding!'

'Not this time, it hasn't.' She laughed as she saw the scepticism on Megan's face. 'Cross my heart and hope to die!'

Megan shook her head. 'Incredible. Still, I am pleased for you, Lucy. I always thought that you and Tom Farrell

had something going. It was obvious from the beginning,'
she added smugly.

'What was obvious?' Lauren demanded, coming into the
office at that moment. Megan lost no time in telling the
other nurse what had happened and Lucy hid her grin. Give
it ten minutes max and the news would be all round the
building!

'What's all the excitement for?' Rob stuck his head
round the door as he heard Lauren's shriek of delight. Lucy
grimaced as Megan launched into the story yet again for
his benefit, obviously getting in some practice before she
regaled everyone else. Rob gave a whoop of delight as he
came into the room and swung Lucy off her feet.

'Brilliant, kiddo! Well done. I thought you and the boss
would never get your act together,' he declared.

'Look who's talking,' she retorted as the other two
women left the room, no doubt intending to spread the glad
tidings further afield.

'If you mean me and Meredith, then that's where you're
wrong.' Rob sounded smug as he saw her surprise. 'We
have finally got things straight—mainly thanks to you and
Tom, I might add.'

'What do you mean?' she queried, puzzled.

Rob sighed. 'That I realised how stupid it was not to try
to sort things out when I saw how upset you and Tom were
after the Blake baby was abducted.' He shrugged. 'It was
obvious that you two needed to talk, but for some reason
you were avoiding it. It just struck me that I was acting
much the same way by not making Meredith explain what
was wrong, so I went round to her flat after I dropped you
off.'

'And?' she prompted, unconsciously holding her breath
as he paused.

'And I found out that she is pregnant, although I believe
she had already told you, hadn't she?' Rob said quietly.

'That's right. So how do you feel about the idea, Rob?'

'Shell-shocked!' he admitted ruefully. He suddenly

grinned. 'But I have to say that I'm adapting to the idea of becoming a dad very quickly!'

'Oh, I'm so pleased for you both! So what happens now? Are there going to be more wedding bells in the not-too-distant future?'

'Let's just say that I'm working on it. Meredith still needs a bit of persuading, but I'm fairly confident that I can convince her that I'm serious,' he said lightly. He glanced round as the door opened and Tom appeared. 'Congratulations, sir. I've just heard the good news about you and Lucy.'

'Thanks, Rob. I hope you'll be able to make it to the wedding? We would like all our friends to be there to help us celebrate.' Tom came further into the room, smiling at her with such love in his eyes that she felt her heart surge. 'We have waited a very long time for this to happen and both of us want to make it a very special occasion.'

'I wouldn't miss it for anything! Nor will most of the hospital, I imagine.' Rob laughed. 'Anyway, I'd better go and make a start.'

He gave Lucy a wink before he hurried out of the room and she chuckled. 'I think Rob was trying to be tactful by letting us have a few minutes together on our own,' she explained when Tom's brows rose questioningly.

'Mmm, seems to me that he might just have a point there.' He drew her into his arms and kissed her hungrily, then laughed ruefully. 'It's only half an hour since I left you and yet it feels like days since I held you in my arms! I wonder what can be wrong with me, Staff Nurse Benson?'

'I'm not really qualified to make a diagnosis, Dr Farrell, but I suspect that it's a bad case of love. Think you'll pull through?'

'Only with a lot of tender loving care,' he growled, pulling her unceremoniously back into his arms. He sighed as he reluctantly let her go. 'Well, I suppose we shall have to start work, although I must confess that it's going to be extremely difficult to keep my mind on my job today. You, Staff Nurse, have a strange effect on my equilibrium.'

'Good!' she declared, laughingly evading him as he made a grab for her again. She headed for the door, then paused when the phone suddenly rang. Tom answered it and she frowned as she tried to piece together the conversation from what little she could hear. He was smiling when he put the receiver back on its rest.

'That was the police,' he explained, following her out into the corridor. 'Evidently, when one of the papers ran the story about Jonathan's abduction they happened to mention that he had been treated at the same hospital where Rosie is being cared for. They did a recap of what had happened and printed the photograph of her mother again. A chap called Brian Hodges has contacted them. He says that he is Rosie's father.'

'No? But that's wonderful news!' They had reached the unit and she led the way straight to Rosie's cot. 'But why didn't he come forward before?'

'Because he has been working in the States for the past five months. He and Rosemary Morrison evidently had some sort of row and split up so he had no idea that she was pregnant. He just happened to see the article in the paper when he was flying home and contacted the police as soon as he landed. Obviously, there will need to be blood tests et cetera, but the police seem to think he is genuine.'

'So she is going to have a family of her own after all. Oh, Tom, it's wonderful news, isn't it? Another miracle in a way?' she declared, a lump coming to her throat as she looked at the tiny baby.

'It is.' He took a deep breath as he looked round the unit. 'I've often thought that each of the babies we manage to save is a small miracle in its own way. But miracles come in all shapes and forms, don't they?'

She knew what he meant and her heart spilled over with love. 'They do. We're so lucky, Tom, aren't we?'

'We are indeed.' He returned her smile with one which

held a wealth of promise. It was an effort to focus on work for the rest of the day but she did her best. However, she wasn't sorry when it was time to go home at last. It had been a strain being around Tom when she had wanted to keep on touching him all the time, but that would have been highly unprofessional!

She collected her coat then hurried downstairs. Tom had said that he would meet her in the foyer and he was there as promised. He had Adam with him and she felt her heart overflow with happiness as the child came running towards her.

She swung him up into her arms and held him close. He was just so precious because he was Tom's son, the child she had longed for and thought she would never have. As she went to join Tom she knew that she was the luckiest woman in the whole world. She had everything she had ever wanted: the man she loved with her whole heart and his child. If she hadn't believed in miracles before, then she believed in them now!

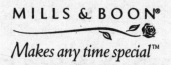

MILLS & BOON®

Makes any time special™

Seduction
GUARANTEED

THE MORNING AFTER *by Michelle Reid*

César DeSanquez wants revenge on Annie Lacey for tearing
his family apart. Sweeping her off to his family island, he
ruthlessly seduces her, only to discover she is innocent…

A WOMAN OF PASSION *by Anne Mather*

In the heat of Barbados, cool Helen Gregory's inhibitions
are melted by Matthew Aitken's hot seduction. But
Matthew seems to be already involved—with Helen's
glamorous mother!

RENDEZVOUS WITH REVENGE
by Miranda Lee

Ethan Grant was Abby's boss—so why had he asked her
to pose as his lover at a weekend conference? Ethan
hadn't let Abby in on his plans, but, once he seduced her
into becoming his real lover, would he tell her the truth?

Look out for **Seduction Guaranteed**
in June 2000